On My Terms

By S G Marshall

This is a work of fiction. Names, characters, businesses, places, events and incidents are either the products of the author's imagination or used in a fictitious manner. Any resemblance to actual persons, living or dead, or actual events is purely coincidental.

Published by S G Marshall
© 2016 S.G. Marshall

Part One

New Beginnings

1

JC Richards calmly exited a train carriage at St Paul's station and consulted his well-worn Rolex watch. He had fallen behind schedule. The interview was secured not so much by his credentials as by his ability to smooth talk Daphne Philips the recruitment consultant at the employment agency. The role of Personal Assistant slash office manager was hardly the occupation of his dreams but the salary was impressive and the terms and conditions suited his needs perfectly. Although unable to foresee the drawbacks he was wily enough to know that somewhere along the line there had to be a catch. But deliberating over negative aspects of the post would have to wait until after he had achieved his objective.

Without further hesitation he jogged majestically along the busy streets. A consistent pace was maintained by projecting exaggerated breathing sounds to herald his presence, and as commuters adjusted their stride to allow safe passage his thoughts turned to those closest to him and in particular Amanda. The JC she first encountered held a simple philosophy when it came to personal relationships; avoid emotional entanglement. He could be spotted most nights at the more salubrious West End bars, with a different woman draped over his arm. He had one type. Smartly dressed, tall slim blondes. High flyers, or at the very least professionally qualified and unashamedly seeking a long-term relationship with their male counterpart. To some extent JC fit the bill. The credentials that virtually guaranteed he would get to first base - eloquent and suave with the ability to make others laugh without really trying – were ably supported by his physical appearance. At 6ft 1ins tall with an athletic physique, undeniable good looks, well-staged thick blonde hair and communicative blue eyes, he was frequently compared to a young Brad Pitt. A stagnant career and lack of academic qualifications did not detract from his charm offensive. Besides he was not averse to lying in order to get his way and conversely, like all good scholars he would go the extra mile to pursue someone or something that intrigued him.

His usual modus operandi was to befriend a malleable senior colleague at his place of work. It was then a simple matter of gaining insight into their area of expertise, hopes and aspiration. On meeting an attractive women he would put all he had learnt into practice. Tastefully playing the role of the go-getter; even mimicking his colleague's mannerisms. Once the night was over and the passion had dissipated the conclusion was always the same. He would see that look in her eyes. The look of hope for the future. The possibility *of a happily ever after*. But there would be no second date. He would not return her calls. The following night would yield a brand-new challenge.

'Why don't you look where you are going?!'
The collision with the elderly pedestrian brought JC back to the present, and all the adverse

emotions associated with an impending interview swiftly returned.

'I'm sorry sir. I should have been looking where I was going.'

JC's response was polite but nonchalant. He tried desperately not to break stride as he spoke and glanced furtively at his watch. Thoughts primarily focused on evading the next passer-by. His lack of sincerity provoked the pedestrian into launching a more vigorous verbal assault, only now it was directed against anyone he considered to be in a hurry to reach their destination.

'There was a time when people looked out for each other and respected their elders' he bellowed.' It did not matter whether they were a friend or stranger..!'

The words struck deep. JC's default position, to be courteous to others was being questioned and for the briefest of moments his instincts wrestled with his desire to reach his destination. It took one more glance at his watch to remind him where his priorities lay. The continued rantings of his accuser now fading into the distance inspired JC to quicken his pace, and within minutes he was standing at the entrance of the interview venue itself. The ultra-modern Wrex Tower building, located in the heart of the City of London.

****

After announcing his arrival to the receptionist there was just enough time to go through his pre-interview ritual. The ground floor gentlemen's toilet proved the ideal location. Unoccupied and well-maintained the elongated wall mirror ensured a head to toe view of his efforts. He began with his face, paying particular attention to his teeth, then fingernails and black brogue shoes. He appropriately adjusted his tie and eventually his newly purchased navy blue suit.

The self-examination ended as it always did, with an assessment of his hair. It was his pride and joy. A former girlfriend once referred to it as his 'mane' due to its length and thickness. It was - he believed - what made him stand out from the crowd, and made new acquaintances perceive him as approachable yet, more importantly, difficult to gauge. He had only recently taken the decision to shorten the length in a bid to appear more contemporary, but it was an integral part of his identity and too valuable a tool to radically alter.

Although satisfied with his appearance it was a troubled expression that peered back at him. Amanda was uncomfortable with his decision to apply for the position. She considered the role to be that of a *glorified secretary* and therefore beneath him. Without her support his confidence was visibly impaired. Though conscious of the detrimental effect she was having on his preparations, she still refused to alter her stance. None of this made sense to him. They were used to living a comfortable lifestyle, surely their energies should be focused on preserving what they have? With her celebrity status on the wane it was vital that he found a position that would help to sustain them for the foreseeable future.

'I should not be feeling this way.......I should not be feeling this way before an interview!'

Though intent on voicing his frustration he had the presence of mind to speak quietly, mindful that one of the cubicles was now occupied. Still peering into the mirror he was surprised to see how much his appearance had altered since his partying days. His features more chiselled conferring a more masculine look. His hands hirsute. But the physical changes were minute in comparison to his psychological transformation. That was a far more unpredictable process which began nearly seven years ago when the most influential person in his life was one Lenny Wiseman.

Lenny was a giant of a man, in almost every sense of the word. He stood at six foot 3 inches tall, with a rotund yet strapping physique, perpetually bronzed appearance and short cropped brown hair. The two men worked together at North Sacs International, a company that specialised in LIBOR based bonds, loan and forfeiting markets.

Lenny had been working at the company for five and a half years when JC was first appointed. During that time he was consistently involved in disputes with management. He was suspected of pilfering office equipment in 2005 but the subsequent investigation was deferred due to lack of evidence. The following year his integrity was again questioned when human resources officially termed his conduct towards a young female colleague as *bordering on harassment*.

William Reeves, the Human Resources Manager was exasperated by his inability to reprimand Lenny, but in his defence he had a formidable opponent. Following his initial confrontation with management Lenny took it upon himself to absorb every scrap of information he could lay his hands on regarding employment law. He would spend his evenings in local libraries mumbling incoherently to himself as he hypothesised scenarios where he would outwit senior managers. It so happened that Lenny's periods of absence often coincided with particularly busy periods for his department, when it was essential that everyone pulled their weight. On returning to work he found himself having to fend off awkward questions regarding his conduct not only from management but also from colleagues he had previously considered friends.

At the exact time that Lenny's popularity had reached its lowest point JC was becoming the *golden boy* of the organisation. His amiable personality and obliging manner enabled him to form positive relationships within a remarkably short period of time. Within three months of his appointment JC was on first name basis with all of the senior management team; his forte being his ability to put strait-laced managers at ease with his wry sense of humour. His *suave* appearance combined with an innate ability to lavish compliments at appropriate times meant that he also accrued numerous female admirers, but he made a point of never going on dates with colleagues. Although he never expressed an interest in rising through the ranks rumours were rife that a superfluous non-executive role would be created to provide him with the experience and knowledge needed for rapid progression.

Given the contrasting popularity of both men it was inevitable that concerns were raised when they developed a friendship that was standing the test of time. The consensus was that Lenny, being six years older than JC, would sway the younger man into behaving in a manner that would prove detrimental to his career.

Initial attempts to impede their relationship were unsuccessful. Chiefly because the two men shared interests that they could only articulate to one another. In effect they needed each other. JC's high regard for Lenny first manifested when he overheard him expressing his views on the discovery of Tutankhamen's burial site in 1922 to perplexed colleagues. Although fascinated by historical facts and archaeological discoveries in particular JC would have been reluctant to engage in such discourse in the past, but he considered Lenny to be of similar ilk to him. A kindred spirit whose desire to convey his opinions and absorb unusual trivia had also remained unfulfilled.

Paradoxically JC's eagerness to converse was further motivated by the fact that Lenny had been ostracised. As a consequence Lenny was unable to belittle his theories to anyone of note at the Company. As their friendship developed JC frequently found himself captivated by Lenny's unique oratory style, and in awe of his extensive general knowledge. His detailed accounts of historical events, which frequently ended with a remarkable and sometimes questionable twist, left him enthralled.

From Lenny's perspective it was almost inconceivable that someone as contemporary and gregarious as JC would want to be associated with him. Lenny was a loner. Forming meaningful long-term relationships had always proved difficult but he was proud to tell anyone who cared to listen how he was briefly engaged to one Bethany Wilkins, a lover of heavy metal music and oriental tattoos. Bethany worked in Lenny's local patisserie store just a stone's throw from Leytonstone tube station in East London. At the time Lenny was renting a one bedroom apartment in Bushwood; the most popular place of residence in the area. The location impressed Bethany and she would regularly sleep over. Sometimes bringing along friends who had no place else to stay.

Lenny suspected that she was having sexual relations with at least one of her male friends, but he had no evidence. It was just a hunch. Their engagement lasted seven weeks. Lenny spent three times as long agonising over why this was the case but could not come up with a rational explanation.

In time he surmised that acquaintances, be it girlfriends or just good mates would inevitably tire of his company so any attempt to behave in a manner that contradicted his basic instincts was pointless. 'Be yourself and whatever will be will be' was his motto. But he uttered those words with less conviction after he befriended JC.

As their friendship developed Lenny took great pleasure in turning up unexpectedly while JC was conversing with colleagues or entertaining a woman at a bar. Standing shoulder to shoulder with his friend at a time when he was at his charismatic best gave him an elevated feeling of self-worth. His attempts to add humour on these occasions often led to an inappropriate comment being uttered and he would be shunned by JC's acquaintances, but never by JC.

Lenny was oblivious to their thinly veiled hostility. He convinced himself that if they liked his best buddy then surely they must like him too. But for the most part he was merely content to be interacting in what he considered to be a deferential manner within a social setting. Something he never truly became accustomed to.

The cynics were correct in their assumption. JC's attitude to work deteriorated significantly as the friendship developed. Misdemeanours such as arriving late for work and failing to meet deadlines became a regular occurrence. Senior management were willing to give him some leeway but his behaviour was being closely monitored.

The turning point came when the two men returned to work over half an hour late, on a sunny but bitterly cold Friday afternoon. It was Lenny who suggested they visit a bar that served real ale. A fully paid up member of CAMRA Lenny was eager to share his extensive knowledge with JC, and encouraged him to sample some of his favourite tipples. On returning to work they touched base in their respective offices before meeting up once again in the designated smoking area, by the car park. They were cheerfully engrossed in conversation when Mr Reeves appeared.

'Look out here comes the head of the Gestapo.'

Lenny's remark and general demeanour made JC wince. It had visibly wounded Reeves, and subsequently set the tone for their encounter.

'Well…. as Head of Human Resources I think I am well within my rights to ask what you are both doing in the smoking area that could constitute Company business?'

To his credit Reeves had instantly regained his composure. He had to. One false accusation or misconstrued remark could provide Lenny with enough ammunition to elude him once again.

'Well Mr Reeves, sir,' Lenny said confidently, 'I believe we are entitled to a cigarette break and if we happen to be talking at the same time… well, I thought you would consider that to be a good thing for staff morale...'

As Lenny taunted his nemesis JC noticed he had become unsteady on his feet, as if he was inebriated yet he could not have been. He had consumed far less alcohol than he could normally tolerate. The diminutive figure of Reeves appeared to curl into a ball as he dipped into his pocket to retrieve a tawdry blue stained cloth which he used to meticulously clean his spectacles.

The pause in the conflict affected JC most of all. Up until that point he was convinced that Lenny would live up to his reputation and talk his way out of trouble. Now he was not so sure. Reeves put away the cloth and peered upwards, directly into the eyes of a weary looking Lenny. He was ready to resume his offensive.

'Well, it has come to my attention that the two of you returned from lunch extremely late and having briefly returned to your desks, subsequently located yourselves here in the designated smoking area for over half an hour. I have not been given a valid answer to my question so I have no other option but to continue this discussion with you both at a later date in a more formal setting.'

JC stood to attention as Reeves turned to face him for the first time since hostilities began.

'Well J…uh.. Mr Richards, you have not said a word so far; is there anything you wish to contribute to the discussion?'
JC stood motionless, unsure of what to say. He wanted to apologise for behaving in such an uncharacteristic manner. He wanted to explain that in recent months it had become difficult for him to differentiate between work and social boundaries, and after all at 24 years of age he was still young enough to learn from his

mistakes. He wanted to convey so much but one glance towards Lenny made him realise that such a response would be perceived as betrayal and that was something he could not do to his friend.

Reeves sighed. Hitherto he had avoided personalising matters but now he found it impossible to hold back his disappointment.

'Do you know Mr Richards, we have recently taken on a number of individuals with huge potential, but of all our aspiring recruits it was you, we believed, who would be the most successful…' He chose his next few words very carefully.

'There is still time for you to turn things around. I hope you do not let yourself…and us down.'

Visibly shaken by Reeves' thinly veiled threat JC struggled to find an appropriate response. Within moments however his attention was drawn towards Lenny, who had been glaring menacingly at Reeves for some time.

It seemed as if Lenny had doubled in size; his fists were clinched and his face crimson red. Without any warning whatsoever Lenny hurtled towards Reeves at a speed that belied his massive form, pinning him against the car park wall. With just one hand around Reeves' throat he succeeded in raising him off the ground. Reeves' feet kicked out uncontrollably as he struggled desperately for air.

The commotion was overheard by the mail room staff and they funnelled swiftly into the loading bay, eager to intervene. But when they observed the huge frame of Lenny effortlessly immobilising Reeves' they all, to a man retreated.

'Don't you dare threaten JC! If you want to threaten anyone then threaten me!'

Lenny's voice raised an octave as he spoke. He was so focused on exacting revenge that he remained oblivious to the crowd that had formed.

Reeves' body went limp and his complexion a stony shade of grey yet he was somehow able to manoeuvre his head so that he could gaze upon a small group of onlookers.

'I...I was not threatening him...' he murmured.

'I...I have witnesses. You will be in trouble... p..p... please.'

JC should have said something. He was the only one present that had a remote chance of reasoning with Lenny, but he was so shocked by the speed and intensity of the assault that he was rendered speechless. Lenny continued his verbal tirade:

'You can do whatever you want with me, I can handle it but if you threaten JC, my best friend you will pay the price. Do you hear me? You will pay!'

Like a wild animal that had tired of toying with its injured prey, Lenny contemptuously relinquished his grip on Reeves and strode dispassionately towards the stairwell; oblivious to the gravity of his actions. Reeves lay motionless.

There was no attempt to revive him. It was as though all present were paralysed with fear, believing that any involvement, no matter the context, would be to their detriment. An inestimable period of time elapsed before any sign of life was detected. Then a loud cough, followed by a few incomprehensible words and the tension was broken. Now Reeves was surrounded from all sides by colleagues eager to provide aid. The harrowing confrontation was finally at an end but the gruelling inquest was only just beginning.

2

JC took the elevator to the 3rd floor where he was met by a man who looked young enough to be attending middle school. He was then taken to a well-lit room that was devoid of paraphernalia save for an elongated table and the appropriate number of chairs. The interview panel consisted of four people, and was headed by the only man on the panel. He was also the youngest interviewer by a considerable number of years.

'Hello Joslin, My name is Marvin Webb, Head of Development. This is Jen Palmer the Senior PA Administrator...'

Marvin turned to Jen and smiled. Although aware of the attention Jen chose to ignore Marvin. Instead her gaze remained fixed on JC, only now she smiled with renewed enthusiasm.

The snub unsettled Marvin and as he shifted uncomfortably in his seat JC was presented with time to inspect his chief inquisitor. Even from a seated position and partially concealed by the table he could tell that Marvin was above average height. He had a slender, almost feminine physique, and short cropped red hair. His narrow cheekbones and elongated nose ensured he would always stand out in a crowd. Marvin continued with the introductions but neglected to mention the job titles of the other panel members, much to their displeasure.

The interview questions were predictable. Similar to the one's JC himself had posed when he was an interviewer, at the height of his hitherto short-lived career. But he was taken back by the flirtatious behaviour of the female panel members, who were neglecting to take notes.

Susan Ainsley, whom he later discovered was the senior policy officer, made no attempt whatsoever to contribute to the process. She merely smiled amorously and nodded whenever JC responded to a question. Beatrice McDermott, the Human Resource Manager took to gently stroking her shoulder length blond hair in a suggestive manner. Occasionally she would giggle to herself for no apparent reason. But it was Jen who was the ring-leader, and every now and then she would up the ante by making a highly suggestive remark that made her previous effort appear tame by comparison.

It was not unusual for an interviewer to flirt with him. He was used to that. It was the combined assault that JC found disconcerting and as the interview progressed he found himself wondering whether he would accept the position when, and not if, it was offered to him.

It seemed that there was only one obstacle to an offer of employment, and that was Marvin. Frustrated by his colleagues' attempts to undermine him and envious of JC's popularity he was finding it increasingly difficult to conceal his disdain for all in attendance. He proceeded to talk over his colleagues; communicating in a brash and occasionally belligerent manner. At one stage his conduct so provoked Susan that she seemed destined to finally say her piece. Having promptly sat up and lifted her gaze towards the ceiling, she slowly parted her lips; but her words were inaudible. It was not until two days later that JC concluded she had uttered the words *God, he is so unprofessional*!

Marvin ultimately succeeded in posing questions that proved problematic. They were the kind of questions that JC would have negotiated with ease under normal interview conditions. But these were not normal conditions:

'Now according to your C.V. you have spent the last 5 years as a house-husband, looking after your two children…. admirable…'

Marvin paused momentarily and as he did so a smile crossed his face. The notion of a talented young man sacrificing his career to nurture offspring seemed both irrational and foolhardy to him. Failing to recall that he had recently been shunned by Jen he turned to face her, hoping to convey his disdain. His gaze was met with a stern expression. This time he was undeterred:

'Although the position has clearly stated hours you will occasionally have to work late in the evenings and at short notice, would this cause difficulties?'

'No….Not Really. No'

'Not really?'

Marvin eased back in his chair, simultaneously folding his arms and stretching out his exceptionally long legs. 'The floor is yours Mr Richards, would you care to elaborate?'

JC had redrafted his CV specifically for the position but neglected to revise his handiwork. He was unable to recall the salient changes relating to child supervision. A cursory glance across the table informed him that the interviewers were aware of his discomfort.

'Would you like a glass of water Joslin?'

'Uh…yes. Thank you Beatrice.'

As JC slowly sipped from the glass he could feel the tension ease from mind and body. His perception of events altered too. It was as if he had become a primed athlete who was being vigorously cheered to the finishing line but struggling to rid himself of his dynamic and highly motivated competitor. If he was to put in a weak finish it would be Marvin and his outmoded notions that would prevail. After thanking Beatrice once again he was ready to reconvene.

'Sorry about the hesitancy. All this talking has left my throat feeling a little dry. Now in answer to your question, I have a number of friends and relatives who could step in at a moment's notice to help with childcare, so it's not a problem.'

This was a lie. There was no-one. JC's family could not be relied upon and he had lost contact with his true friend's long before his paternal instincts kicked in. There were similar concerns with his partner's connections. Most of her relatives lived abroad, or in other parts of the United Kingdom. And as for her friends? They were more suited to partying the night away than reading bedtime stories to children.

JC's reply was spoken with enough conviction to deter additional probing, but Marvin was determined to maintain the level of intensity.

'I assume you have thoroughly read the job description and personal specification?'

'Yes'

'Good. Then you will no doubt understand that this is a unique role unlike any other within the organization. What can you bring to the role that is *unique*?'

Unable to come up with a snappy response JC knew it was important not to appear hesitant for a second time. In desperation he resorted to humour.

'Unique,' he said confidently, 'you mean apart from my amazing good looks and sparkling personality.'

The room fell silent. A bemused expression presided over Marvin's face. He had no idea how to negotiate the candidate's unorthodox riposte. Jen looked anxiously towards Beatrice, who met her gaze with a quizzical expression. Suddenly and quite unexpectedly it was Susan who broke the silence.

'Now that's exactly what we need around here; a man who does not take himself too seriously.'

Almost as one the female panellists burst into fits of laughter, while Marvin looked down at his notes, shook his head and shifted uncomfortably in his chair.

****

Following the interview Jen provided JC with a tour of the building. The process was taking longer than he anticipated. He'd skipped breakfast that morning and as a consequence was beginning to experience hunger pangs when they came to the main event.

'... and this is the office of the line manager for the vacant position, who is also one of the directors of the company. Your office, should you be offered the position, is next door. '

'Wow, my own office. Not bad for a PA position.'

JC's flippant remark led to his first adverse response from a female panel member.

'It is a combined PA and office manager's position Mr Richards! A highly respected role within the organisation and you will do well to remember that.'

JC hoped to redeem himself by commenting favourably on Jen's interview technique but was distracted by the condition of the line manager's office. It was the only one on the 3rd floor not to have a name plaque on the door. Inside, it was devoid of personal photos and all those other unobtrusive yet intimate knick-knacks that have the capacity to turn a dreary, soulless environment into an effective motivational tool.

He thought how strange it was that he had yet to set eyes on the Director. He had never known a line manager to deliberately miss out on the selection process for their closest assistant. Their ego combined with the desire to instantly define working parameters took precedence over other pressing matters. It was almost too embarrassing to pose the question at this late stage but after mulling it over for a few minutes he considered it necessary to do so.

'So, what is the name of the Director that I will be working for? That is assuming I was offered the position of course.' Jen appeared to be flustered by the question.

'Oh yes, about that; she apologises profusely for being unable to attend…unavoidable…a business trip to Milan. Rest assured we will be giving her a comprehensive account of today's proceedings, so she will still have a key part to play in the selection process.'

He had already committed one faux pas during his tour it would have been unwise to press the issue and commit another. Besides two valuable pieces of information could be gleaned from Jen's reply. Firstly the director was a woman and secondly, she had tremendous faith in the judgment of her colleagues. These were factors that could be used to his advantage.

Jen escorted JC back to the Lobby where they said their good-byes. By now she had reverted back to being the jovial character whose vibrant energy and strength of character so dominated the morning's proceedings. They shook hands and as they did so Jen gently placed her other hand on his shoulder. She waited until JC had returned her gaze before speaking softly, almost inaudibly, so that no-one else could hear her words.

'I must say your interview appeared to go very well indeed and your C.V. was by far the best of all the candidates.....' She hesitated for a moment then, still firmly clasping his hand moved closer to whisper in his ear.

'I can't say for sure but between you and I...well....it does seem pretty much in the bag!'

She let go of his hand and as if to reassure him bequeathed a lingering smile. He should have been delighted by her words. In some ways he was. But there was something about the way she spoke. The look in her eyes. It all seemed somewhat familiar, but not necessarily in a good way.

The subsequent walk to the train station was riddled with doubts. He had seen this kind of in-fighting before. Two disparate factions on an interview panel, each having made up their mind regarding the candidate's suitability before a question had been posed. He could no longer tolerate the notion that his skills, previous experience and desire to fulfil his potential were irrelevant. But the real contest for the vacant position had taken place on the other side of the finely crafted oak table, and the combatants' decision making process would be heavily influenced by the candidate's outward appearance as well as pre-existing political machinations.

In the future the battleground will no doubt be transferred to meeting rooms and even the boardroom of the organisation, but today collateral damage had been done. And the victims? They were the unknowing interviewees who had woken up that morning having thoroughly prepared for the day's eventualities believing they would be given an equal opportunity to achieve their objective.

***

JC was in need of a haven and there was only one place that would suffice. So after going home to change into more comfortable attire he took a trip to the *Raison d'etre Café*, which was located a mere five minutes walking distance away. Its name was the only aspect of the establishment to even remotely resemble the French dining experience. The menu was unashamedly predisposed to an assortment of *all day English breakfasts* and the staff were of English and Eastern European origin.

It wasn't much to look at either. The façade was composed mostly of glass. Its wooden framework painted an unusual shade of red at some stage in the last five years, but it had been applied so poorly that the previous shade, a glossy sea blue, re-emerged in various places to compete for visual supremacy. The lopsided mustard brown awning displayed a gaping hole that gave the illusion of minutely increasing in size whenever he gazed in its direction. It was also the reason for the deafening sound that could be heard when heavy rainfall descended.

But there was a plus side. Its dilapidated exterior deterred the type of customers that had a habit of commanding his attention. Such as the well-groomed male administrators who thrived on talking loudly on his mobile phone. Gesticulating wildly for no apparent reason while openly comparing his dress sense to that of the other male customers, or the amorous young secretary trying to appear older than her years and forever taking sneaky peaks at him from behind her menu.

JC strolled into the Café undetected in his favourite baggy grey tracksuit bottoms and shabby sky blue t-shirt. He was looking forward to sharing some light-hearted banter with Gloria, the Café manager but instead he was eventually greeted by the waitress.

'Hello, Mr Richards, how can I be helping you?' He was surprised that Natalya was still employed at the café. None of the previous incumbents had lasted more than a week.

'I'll have the usual please, Natalya'.

'The usual….?' She stood motionless, unsure how to respond. His willingness to put an end to her discomfort was exceeded by his fascination with her inability to cope with a simple request.

'Er ….the usual.' As Natalya repeated the words he detected a change in both the tone of her voice and her appearance. Her skin turned pale and the corners of her lips protruded to reveal heavily stained and misaligned lower teeth. Within seconds her left eye began twitching uncontrollably. It was only when he noticed a tear trickle down her left cheek that he intervened.

'There's no need to get upset Natalya. I thought you would have known what my usual is by now, but I imagine only Gloria knows that. I'll have a cappuccino and a slice of Eccles cake…oh, and can you bring the sugar bowl over please.'

'Uh…… of course.' Natalya responded in a servile manner, bowing her head as though addressing royalty before scurrying behind the counter and into the back room.

JC stared soberly at his reflection in the Café window, clarifying his thoughts. Some might say he had treated her dreadfully but he convinced himself otherwise. After all Natalya had addressed him by his surname. How could she have known his surname? They were on first name terms only. He always paid in cash, so she could not have acquired the information from his debit card. Then there was her subordinate behaviour towards him. But it was not just Natalya; her predecessors had also responded to him that way. But on the rare occasions that other customers strayed onto the premises the service they received was so tardy that it virtually guaranteed they would never return.

'Well hello dearie, how are you today?'

Gloria's customary salutation and cheery disposition proved a welcome distraction from his troubled thoughts. She was ever the vivacious host in his presence, and he in turn enjoyed harmlessly flirting with her. A tactile woman with pleasant features Gloria always sported a beehive hairstyle and rectangular black rimmed glasses that complimented her rotund face and slightly overweight physique. She stood at 5ft 7 inches tall in her heels and always dressed smartly underneath her pinafore. It was impossible to guess her age. Gloria's demeanour was that of someone in their mid-forties but her eagerness to initiate discourse on topics such as mobile phone applications and the latest pop chart songs led him to believe that she might be of a younger generation.

During their verbal exchanges JC conversed in the same way that he did with every other women save Amanda; by telling half-truths. In that way he could retain control of their emerging friendship. He spoke of his relationship with his partner as though it was a casual thing. He mentioned his children but neglected to mention key details about them. Their interests, how they were getting on at school, or even the fact they were twins.

He always neglected to mention the kind of information that turned a female acquaintance into a true friend.

'So how did the interview go dearie?' He had informed Gloria of his interview date over a week ago but did not think for a minute that she would remember.

'I think it went well.'

'I'm sure it did.' She hummed chirpily, oblivious to the negativity surrounding his response.

'Now, how about I go bring you your order and we can gabble some more.'

'Thanks Gloria and can you also bring me a sugar...' Gloria immediately took a sugar bowl from the counter and placed it on the table. By the time she returned with his order JC was feeling upbeat for the first time that day and consequently spoke without administering his usual discretion.

'I'm not sure what Natalya is doing, she appears to be at sixes and sevens today!'

'What do you mean?' The tone of Gloria's voice immediately changed.

'Oh, don't worry Gloria. Everything is fine now that the calories have arrived! Do you get it *calories* instead of cavalry?'

His attempt to lighten the mood had no bearing whatsoever. This was a side to Gloria that he had not seen before. Her steely gaze compelled him to respond appropriately to her question.

'It's just that she seemed a little more nervy than usual........ unsure of my order, but I'm sure it's a one-off. She really is great to have around.'

'Oh, she is.' Gloria's cheery disposition returned.

'She probably has something on her mind, poor thing. I'll have a chat with her. Maybe I can help her in some way.'

They exchanged smiles. JC was genuinely relieved that he had retrieved the situation but as Gloria turned to go back into the kitchen he noticed her facial expression change once more. An ominous scowl emerged that sent a shiver down his spine. It was not visible for long, just the briefest of moments. But still long enough for him to realise that Natalya would no longer be employed at the 'Raison d'etre Café by the end of the day.

3

It was a wet and humid Friday; the time 5.35pm. Ordinarily the lads would have assembled in the lobby by now with Jackets dangling over their shoulders and beaming smiles on their faces, whispering to each other like excited schoolboys who were privy to an inestimable conundrum which all but guaranteed an enthralling night ahead. Their chosen venue that evening was the fashionable 'Hydration' nightclub in Bond Street, central London.

An hour before their scheduled rendezvous *Print Room* Pete, the newest recruit to their boy's nights out sent a text to his friends. He was unable to put in an appearance that evening; he did not elaborate. Thirty minutes later JC received a call from Lenny. His line manager needed his help on an urgent matter that might take some time, but he would join him at the venue as soon as possible.

JC suspected this was all part of a conspiracy by management to prevent them from socialising. Ever since Lenny's altercation with Reeves the pressure on the two men to sever their friendship had gained momentum. But they could still consider themselves fortunate. As punishment for his misdemeanour Lenny was given his first written warning and *persuaded* to work longer hours. JC was given a verbal warning. When JC asked Lenny how he managed to avoid facing criminal charges and instant dismissal he received a cryptic response.

'Let's just say you are not the only one with friends in high places.' JC took this to mean that other, unspecified conditions were imposed which Lenny was too embarrassed to divulge.

Forty five minutes had passed and JC was still standing on his own at the night club. Deprived of his wing man he would have departed long ago were it not for a woman he noticed glancing in his direction from time to time. She had sparked his curiosity chiefly because of her conduct rather than her appearance. She was standing close to the dance floor, flanked by her companions who were evidently having a wonderful time yet she chose to remain on the periphery of their exchanges. Unwilling to participate yet clearly at ease with the situation.

This was her opening gambit. A pattern of behaviour he all too frequently adopted in order to get his own way. In JC's case it usually led to concerns being raised that *he was not his usual self*, and once he had become the centre of attention he would eagerly dictate the topics that were up for discussion.

It was both a challenging and conceited thing to do and whilst he had no qualms about executing such a strategy he could not imagine that this inappropriately dressed, wholesome young woman would be adept enough to carry it off.

It took a while before all eyes were drawn to her but moments after gaining their attention her companions were treated to an amusing anecdote. Some began mimicking her mannerisms. One person gently clapped his hands. A sure sign that she was firmly in control. Astounded by her clinical execution JC edged closer to the group, and when it seemed that she was about to deliver yet another quip he stood directly behind her companions to gauge their response. In that same instant she paused, looked directly at him and delivered an engaging smile.

The glance towards him at such a key moment in her monologue ensured that all eyes followed her gaze. What a marvellous strategy! To her companions it seemed that even passing strangers were susceptible to her charms. No doubt she would gain kudos from this. One day he may look back at her theatrics with admiration, but at that moment in time he felt like the proverbial rabbit caught in the glare of an oncoming vehicle's headlights. Her surprisingly melodic voice was a welcome relief from the impasse.

'We appear to have an interloper in our midst but all are welcome. Hi my name is Amanda.'

'Oh, uh…Hi, I'm JC.'

A few words. That was all it took for him to deduce that Amanda was well-versed and with an affluent background. Once again this was not what he had expected. Ignoring the persistent giggling of her companions Amanda painstakingly introduced each one of them to him. Within seconds her companions had made a hasty retreat to the bar, ostensibly with the intention of providing JC and Amanda with an opportunity to become better acquainted. The situation seemed almost surreal to him. Amanda's companions and even Amanda herself were convinced he would attempt to seduce her.

JC was indeed in the company of someone he found intriguing but she did not possess the panache that was synonymous with his usual conquests. Seemingly aware of his ambivalence Amanda met his gaze with an anxious smile.

It was the first time that thoughts of absent friends or Amanda's lively companions did not impede their interaction. He noticed that Amanda was not wearing make-up. Her tedious hairstyle - blond hair positioned indolently in a ponytail - flagrantly exposed her beautifully sculptured face. Her exquisitely shaped nose and full lips, which pouted suggestively each time she giggled were surpassed only by her ubiquitous blue eyes, which seemed to converse on a level that was beyond his limited comprehension, yet generously permitted feelings of excitement and optimism to surge within him.

'Shall we go to the bar and get a drink, or would you rather move to the dance area?'

The way Amanda spoke and the composure she exhibited as she lead him onto the dance floor implied that intimacy was inevitable. It seemed futile to resist. He admired Amanda's self-confidence and holding hands with her - a mode of conduct that had always seemed unnatural to him - now felt ordained. But as soon as she released her grip the spell was broken and JC returned to type. He took a step back from her in order to soak in the atmosphere and survey the dance floor.

It was JC's first visit to the Hydration Nightclub and he was becoming annoyed with himself for not adhering to his usual routine. On arrival at an unfamiliar venue he preferred to stroll around with a drink in hand, identifying the habitats of the most attractive woman; where they congregated and the best places to make-out. He would end the evening in the company of the most attractive female available or no-one at all. This night would end differently because he found himself liking Amanda; a lot. And did not wish to upset her. Nevertheless like a male peacock instinctively strutting in anticipation, he could not help but speculate.

Amanda danced seductively; gazing down at her movements, ostensibly in admiration of her own artistic ability. She occasionally looked up at JC, hoping for endorsement, which he dutifully dispensed in the form of a smile or a humorous comment. Amanda failed to notice a flame haired woman standing close by who was locked in an intimate embrace with her date. The woman could not keep her eyes off of JC and for his part, JC could see no harm in entering the fray.

More than anything it was the attention that he craved and he relished the fact that her exaggerated movements, as she ran her fingers through her lover's hair and caressed the base of his neck were enacted for the sole purpose of establishing a connection with him. He had first-hand experience of such women. Women who were preoccupied with the notion that unrestrained physical intimacy borne from heightened expectations was the most intense kind. Her attentive and visibly older partner was merely the bait that would help her lure the real prize. Him. Or someone like him.

Amanda's hand gently brushed along JC's arm, establishing that he was not alone. A startled expression promptly appeared on the woman's heavily tanned face. She seemed personally offended by Amanda's attire; the pink baggy tracksuit bottoms, purple jumper and black trainers. She remonstrated by shaking her head and muttering words that were imperceptible over the intensity of the music.

Her sudden movements revived her apathetic partner who responded by whispering incessantly into her ears. They then proceeded in the direction of the bar. She made a point of avoiding eye contact with JC.

Up until that moment JC had found the unpredictability of the night intriguing, but it had now reached new levels of discomfort. He would have no more of it.

'Look Amanda, it's been lovely to meet you but I'm afraid that I have to leave. I've just remembered something that I urgently need to do.'

It took a while before his terse words were processed but then a look of disbelief consumed Amanda's tender features. She made a vain attempt to turn away, as if to join her friends at the bar but realising how foolish she might appear to them she decided to stand her ground; contemplate her next move. There was no point in him denying there was an instant rapport between them and, while he was not sure how he hoped their liaison would end, it was not like this. He decided to do something that he had never done before on a first encounter. JC dipped into his jacket pocket and pulled out a card.

'Uh…here's my number and e-mail address… perhaps we can go for a meal sometime?'

Amanda made no attempt to resume eye contact. Instead she looked disdainfully at the card and subsequently averted her gaze towards a group of women whose crooning had reached a volume that had become annoying to other revellers. JC walked swiftly towards the exit but before he reached his destination he turned to take one last look at his able host. She was gone.

As JC walked slowly towards Bond Street tube station all he could think of were his verbal exchanges with Amanda.

'How could I have led her on like that? She seemed like such a nice girl.' A passing couple overheard his heartfelt soliloquy and broke off from their embrace to provide him with a measured smile. It was as if they wanted to convey their sympathies but feared that verbalising those concerns could lead to hostilities. He failed to notice the couple. What troubled him most of all was how impossible it was to categorise his encounter with Amanda.

She was not his usual prey, nor was she the type of person he would usually look to for friendship, as entertaining as she was. No, she was far too capable of stealing the limelight. A relationship between them would have to commence on an emotional level that he had not yet encountered, and that was a frightening supposition.

His thoughts were disrupted by the vibrating of his mobile phone. He was in the habit of placing it on silent mode when out on the town so whoever was calling could have been trying to get through to him for some time. Was it Amanda calling him already? If so, what will he say to her?

'Hello………oh, Lenny how are you mate? No I decided to leave the bar. I felt like going home early….yes, I'm alone for a change. What happened tonight? Not a lot really. It was surprisingly quiet ……. Okay, I'll give you a call tomorrow.'

****

The time was 5.45pm and his date was already 15 minutes late. At least she had chosen an excellent venue. A prestigious, newly opened bar and restaurant located in Muswell Hill, his favourite London suburb. It had been arranged at short notice. At the time of receiving her call JC was having a conversation with Lenny. They were standing beside the defective first floor photocopier discussing the origins of braille writing. When Lenny realised that the call was from one of JC's conquests he did his upmost to distract him; pulling faces and making unconvincing animal sounds. Once the phone call was over he was eager to hear all the details.

'I'm just meeting a good friend. Nothing more.'

'Right…. Yeah… a good friend. A female friend? I've got news for you *Don Juan* you do not have *good* female friends.' Lenny only referred to JC as Don Juan on those rare occasions when he thought he was withholding *valuable* information.

'What's this er…. friend of yours called then?'

At that precise moment Print Room Pete arrived to fix the photocopier. Once greetings were exchanged JC attempted to engage Pete in general conversation, but Lenny was having none of it.

'Focus Don Juan …. I asked you a question, and I have yet to receive an answer. What is her name?!'

'Aucune edée, je suis désolé.' JC took to conversing in French whenever Lenny broached a subject he was uncomfortable with; it usually put him off his stride. He first discovered Lenny's aversion to foreign languages while on a night out in Stratford, East London soon after they became close friends. On that occasion they approached two women at a bar and after an uncomfortable start everything seemed to be going smoothly. JC was about to demonstrate he could count to ten in Japanese when Lenny delivered an unexpected tirade.

'Foreign languages are a ridiculous waste of time,' he snapped. 'One day everyone will be talking in English so why don't they all just get on with it and learn to speak the Queen's English now!'

Not long after his outburst the two women, who were Italian foreign exchange students made their excuses and left. JC surmised that Lenny had responded so vehemently because foreign languages provided the one gap in his reservoir of knowledge that he was unable or unwilling to address. Nothing he had heard or seen since then had convinced him otherwise. Fortunately for JC the strategy proved effective once again.

'Okay Don Juan I've got to go. Some of us have important work to do, but I want to hear all about it after the event. If you get my drift.'

JC had his reasons for not wanting to reveal details of his assignation. For one he was not sure where the relationship was heading. But there was another more troubling concern. Since Lenny's disciplinary hearing had taken place the parameters of their friendship had altered. Lenny had to change his attitude, that much was certain. But they no longer went for lengthy cigarette breaks and their ad hoc chats in the corridor or by the photocopier were a rarity. In short he was becoming boring! But what was most damaging of all was that he neglected to make an appearance at their recently scheduled Friday night clubbing session. If he was no longer going to be a reliable wingman then he should not automatically assume that he will receive all the benefits that goes with it.

JC had now been waiting over an hour for his date to arrive. During that time he consumed a bowl full of savoury peanuts which were washed down with a bottle of high quality chardonnay. He could not decide who he was most annoyed with, his non-show date or the smug maître d' who refused to relinquish eye contact after being told – for the third time by JC – that he was not ready to order.

The only crumb of solace open to him was the endless stream of desirable women entering the establishment. They emerged in a variety of shapes and sizes but all were elegantly dressed, each one seemingly more beautiful than the last. To amuse himself JC decided to match each woman with the man he thought best suited her. Just as he thought the women could not get any lovelier a vision of unparalleled beauty made an entrance which all but took his breath away. She was tall, slightly taller than him in her high heels, and wore a figure hugging knee length black dress which accentuated her deep blue eyes and untamed blond curly locks.

'Wow, this one definitely suits me!' he whispered. She noticed him staring and smiled in a way that made him grateful he was seated, otherwise his legs would most surely have given way. As she was about to saunter by, no doubt to be seated beside her extremely fortunate and successful partner, he felt a sudden urge to reach out and grab her by the arm. To tell her that no matter how long he searched he would never again set eyes upon someone so adorable.

JC prepared himself as best he could for her departure from his line of vision, but to his surprise she halted in front of him. Perhaps he thought, to await vocal appreciation of her splendour before going on her way. He looked up into her eyes. It was only then that a uniquely intense yet strangely familiar emotion welled within him. A feeling of not being in control of what was about to happen or what will happen in the future. Then it suddenly dawned on him. Her faultless features, the hypnotic way that she moved and the irrepressible smile that could light up a darkened room. It could only be one person.

'Oh my God. It's my date…...Amanda!'

4

JC carefully tip-toed his way through the trail of biscuit crumbs and LEGO bricks which terminated at the oak front door so that he could observe the twins greeting their mother. As they hugged her tightly and recounted the highlights of their day he remained on the periphery, hoping to gauge her mood.

The fact that Amanda did not acknowledge his presence was testament to her current state of mind, not his. To the outside world the relationship between them was as strong as ever. Still the perfect couple who were keeping a low profile for now but eventually, when the time was right, they would take the country by storm again. As he returned to the kitchen to monitor their evening meal JC remained positive about their future. After all they both knew where the problem lay and once you know that then half the battle is already won.

It was unusual for Amanda to join him in the kitchen prior to supper, but on this occasion he was not surprised. She still had the children in tow but they were less boisterous, distracted by the gleaming BMW key ring that was firmly secured to her belt loop. The sombre expression etched on her face convinced him that she was in need of solace and willing to open up a little. So, after encouraging the children to retreat to the sitting room he poured Amanda a glass of her favourite tipple.

'Ohhh.... thanks JC. Well, how was your day?'

She was referring to his interview of course, but he feigned ignorance in order to establish her true level of interest.

'I've had a strange day. Lots of ups and downs.'

'Not with anyone I know I hope!'

Her attempt at humour and the lingering smile that followed were the clearest indications yet that she was starting to unwind. It was the kind of retort that was synonymous with Amanda during their courtship, and what he missed most of all in their relationship. He hoped to maintain the level of joviality.

'I'll have you know that I have been the perfect gentleman today. I dressed stylishly and minded my p's and q's.'

'Dressed stylishly?' Amanda could not help but laugh before delivering her punchline, 'Even at your best you couldn't get a date at London Zoo.'

Now they were both laughing hysterically.

'You know full well that I had an interview this morning and, if you must know I had the panel eating out of the palm of my hands…ah, now it does sound like I spent the day at London Zoo.'

They conversed light-heartedly on a variety of subjects for a time. Inevitably the conversation returned to his interview.

'….it was a strange experience to say the least. I thought it was a done deal but just before leaving I was told that the chosen candidate would be contacted before the end of the working day. Well...' He glanced up at the kitchen clock,

'It's getting quite late now so it's not likely to be me.'

'Well you never know' she replied. 'Do you remember when I applied for my current job? It took them two days to get back... to....'

She could not bring herself to complete the sentence. Deliberating on her place of employment served only to remind Amanda why she had been so despondent prior to their amusing banter.

What concerned him most of all was her blank expression. He had seen that look before but on the faces of vagrants as they wandered aimlessly through the less salubrious parts of London. Having lost all hope; no longer caring if they existed in this world or the next. But could things really be so bad for Amanda? If the problem laid solely with her career then why was she having so much difficulty in expressing how she feels? Unless there was another more pressing matter that he was not aware of. He felt utterly hopeless in the face of such adversity.

Concerned for her wellbeing JC followed Amanda out of the kitchen but deferred at the sitting room door when he observed her hugging Jacob. Their son was the one person blessed with the ability to immediately alleviate her anxiety. Jacob appeared vaguely aware of his status. To his credit he always responded in the appropriate manner. On this occasion by

46

repeatedly saying *love you mummy* and gently stroking her hair. JC continued his vigil. Remaining silent, motionless, so as not to intrude on such a poignant scene.

Feeling the need to do more for his mother Jacob stood on the sofa and bent his knees so that he could look her squarely in the eyes. He kissed her tenderly on the nose and then hugged her. Amanda's hair, which had recently been dyed auburn appeared dull and lifeless in comparison to his free-flowing blonde locks. Every time Jacob repositioned his head on her shoulder the thick strands of his hair seemed to slither like the tentacles of an octopus brazenly attempting to secure a firm grip on an inanimate object.

'Mummy loves you too... Mummy loves you so much Tiger'. Tears trickled down her cheeks, but these were tears that heralded inner-contentment rather than sorrow. The mood was irrevocably changed by Louise dashing into the room and enquiring on the whereabouts of her favourite teddy bear. But Amanda's frame of mind remained positive and mother and offspring played happily while JC resumed his duties in the kitchen.

***

Now that his concerns were fading JC allowed his mind to wonder. To reflect on Amanda's true nature. He would never have imagined that the Amanda who waited patiently to be recognised on their first date in Muswell Hill would one day be beset with self-doubts. On that occasion she simply oozed confidence and was eager to converse on any subject he cared to mention. He smiled to himself when recalling their first conversation that night. It was typical Amanda.

'Yes, it's me handsome. This is more or less how I usually look when out on the town. It's an improvement don't you think?'

'Well, yes…definitely. Why were you dressed informally on Friday?'

He got up to help Amanda with her chair but was beaten to the task by the maître d'. Sensing tension between the two men, Amanda waited until the maître d' had departed before responding to the question.

'I went to the gym after work on Friday and had every intention of going straight home afterwards, but I received a call from Ann-Marie. She persuaded me to go for a drink. Do you remember Ann-Marie? Tall with short auburn hair… she would not stop giggling.'

'Oh….yes…yes'.

'I had every intention of going home after the one drink but something made me stay. Perhaps it was the feeling of being liberated. The only woman not making an effort to look good. And then I met you and all I wanted to do was rush home and change. I'm surprised and flattered that you even noticed me.'

He could not help but smile at the irony. Amanda's appearance was key to him noticing her but it was also what eventually drove him away.

'You have a nice smile JC. I bet you must have been told umpteen times that you look like a young Brad Pitt. Did you see him in *Thelma & Louise*?' He was really handsome back then. Just like you. He was also really muscly too, just like…well…, at least you have similar features'.

She was teasing of course. Which made it all the more difficult for him to process what was happening. Yes, he was a hypocrite but in his defence he had been willing to give their relationship a try. He assumed that by the end of the night he would – at best – have made a life-long friend. Amanda still had the same wonderful sense of humour, unquestionable intellect and boundless energy that was on show a few days ago, yet the remarkable change in her outward appearance, and how it made him feel, irrevocably altered the dynamics of their relationship. She had in effect become what he considered to be the 'complete package' and for the first time in his life he was unsure how to proceed.

JC needed a distraction from the unexpected emotions that threatened to overwhelm him, so he focused on what he knew best; people. He juxtaposed the seamless tide of patrons arriving at the establishment with the continuous flow of beverages being consumed and wondered why the proprietor had not simply dispensed with conventional drinking vessels. Surely a more practical solution to their insatiable thirst would be for patrons to form an orderly cue in the wine cellar!

The type of clientele now present in the establishment had altered since his arrival, from the cumbersome carefree business folk to amorous couples. He hastily deduced that most of the patrons footing the bill for the evening were masters of their own destiny. On any given day they could stroll into work late or not at all without having to face recrimination. Their glamorous companions, predominantly younger and female, could achieve limited autonomy and a comfortable lifestyle if they successfully utilised their undeniable charms. Perhaps starting tonight.

A chilling thought occurred to him. Here he was judging others when his own past intentions have been questionable. Had he not always been drawn to a particular kind of women? Professional or at least well educated with a relatively affluent lifestyle? Perhaps he too was looking for a benefactor. Someone who could lavish him with fast cars, Rolex watches and frequent holiday's in the Caribbean. His thoughts were interrupted by Amanda, who was clearly used to receiving more attention from her dates.

'I hope you are okay with going Dutch? Hate it when a man goes all macho on me and wants to pay for everything'.

'I couldn't agree more'.

'Oh,' she said perkily 'I took a cab to get here as I did not want to arrive too late and…..' He felt compelled to intervene.

'Well, if this is evidence of you trying to get here on time then I must remember to pack a camping bed and a thermos full of cocoa for our next date.'

'Yes, well...' she said coyly, 'my apologies. Women's prerogative and all that. Anyway, as I was saying before I was rudely interrupted, as I had to pay an extortionate amount of money for the cab fare to get here I have decided to take the bus home. It's your responsibility to make sure that I get to the bus stop in one piece and *well before* the last bus to High Barnet. Do you think you could manage that?'

'Oh, I think I can do that'. Although brandishing an impish expression and shuffling uncomfortably in his seat Amanda detected sincerity in his voice, and relaxed just that little bit more.

As the evening progressed JC found himself recounting tales of previous conquests. It was the type of information he had previously shared with one other person; Lenny, and only after they had succumbed to the truth serum more commonly known as *several shots of tequila*. It was as though he was hoping to attain absolution for past misdemeanours so that he could begin anew in an untainted and unconstrained relationship. The gamble paid off. Amanda appreciated his candour and responded by being frank about her past relationships and future aspirations.

She spoke of her extensive academic achievements, including a first class honours degree in environmental sciences. She received her chartered meteorologist accreditation two and a half years ago and subsequently taken up a position as a meteorologist at the Met Office. Occasionally working as a broadcast meteorologist for the BBC. Amanda's burning ambition was to establish herself as a regular on National television, and who knows where that might lead.

In an attempt to express the true extent of her aspirations Amanda spoke of her values in rhetoric that still resonates with him to this day:

> 'We are all born with limited abilities but our potential is immense. You are clearly an intelligent and, dare I say it, good looking man who could probably twist anyone around your little finger. If you were to challenge yourself you would be surprised at what you are capable of achieving. Always remember that it is important to take advantage of those periods in life when you are popular because the opportunity to achieve success is fleeting.'

Until those words were spoken JC had been reasonably content with life. The role of an administrator being the full extent of his career ambitions. In fact ever since the altercation with management his focus was solely on remaining employed, even if it meant having to accept a lower grade position. But he was still well liked by influential people at North Sacs and in the coming months he would use Amanda's inspiring words and their blossoming relationship as inspirational tools to achieve new found career objectives.

At the time he did not fully understand the magnitude of his decision. He never considered that in order to achieve these objectives his old yet much loved lifestyle, and even old friends would have to be sacrificed.

****

JC was more relaxed than usual for the day after an interview. Perhaps because there was no need to spend countless hours agonizing over what he did or did not do wrong. The decision had already been made and no doubt the successful candidate informed. In truth it was not only Amanda who had reservations regarding the PA aspects of the role. He had often reflected on how easy it was to distinguish a manager from their PA. Even on social occasions such as office parties, the PA is always on edge. Mindful that they could be called on to perform disparate tasks - some challenging while others menial and occasionally degrading - at a moment's notice.

However, there was another less obvious reason for his positive frame of mind. He was finally coming to terms with the twins attending full time education. Other parents had warned him how the first week without the children in tow would be heart-breaking for a stay at home parent. It had taken three weeks. Three weeks of having to wake the children up early in the morning, when they were still tired and struggling to adapt to a different routine. Three weeks of ensuring that they were properly dressed, had eaten enough food to sustain them until lunchtime and that their book bags and lunch boxes were appropriately stocked. Three weeks of painstakingly separating them from the one person they had relied upon for solace every single day since their birth. It was now the fourth week of term and JC had a different mind-set. He was grateful to be able to do the basic things on his own again such as going for walks or perusing in the local library. On this occasion he decided to take the scenic route to the café, thus avoiding the Eden venture play area.

The Café had just opened its doors, and a new member of staff was waiting to take his order. Instead of 'nervy' Natalya there was a shorter, stouter and more amiable assistant. She introduced herself as Nadia, and told him that she was originally from Rumania. But JC had no intention of referring to her by name or communicating on a personal level. That way she was less likely to lose her job. Eventually Gloria appeared from one of the back rooms.

'Hi Gloria. It's incredible how I can set my watch by you.'

'What do you mean?' Gloria seemed taken back by his comment. There was an uncomfortable silence.

'Oh, it's just that you always surface from behind the counter roughly ten minutes after I arrive and oddly enough, slightly out of breath'.

'There's nothing odd about it. I have 'fingers in a lot of pies' as they say. Always on the go. But the main thing to remember is that I always get the job done. Still, I suppose you are probably used to leaving women breathless instead of finding them in that condition.'

JC was surprised by both the content and venom of Gloria's remark. Nevertheless he went against all instinct and smiled politely. Gloria had become more defensive since the Natalya episode. The fun factor was fast disappearing from their friendship, which was usually his queue to find somewhere new to spend his free time. A solemn expression unexpectedly arose on Gloria's face. There was something that she needed to say and her hesitancy made JC concerned that it might be of a personal nature.

'Uh....have you had any feedback from yesterday's interview?' The look of relief on his face was impossible to mask.

'Oh, No...... and to be honest it is probably for the best. I'll just have to put it down to experience and move on.'

He had hoped to avoid the subject and considered Gloria astute enough to appreciate that fact. Unfortunately for him she was a woman on a mission.

'You're just saying that because you think you haven't got it. You never know though. It's never over until it's over'.

Gloria stood motionless in front of him. A look of contentment gradually extended across her face. Unnerved by the attention JC slowly reached for the sugar bowl before meticulously adding an extra spoonful of sugar to his cappuccino. He noticed that Gloria was wearing high quality designer shoes. Her hairstyle and make-up were presented in a professional manner too.

'Ah, more customers,' exclaimed J.C, relieved that he would no longer be the centre of attention. An elderly couple entered the premises mumbling inaudibly to each other as they surveyed the timeworn furnishings. Seemingly perturbed by the ambience they were either too polite or too embarrassed to make a hasty retreat. JC and Gloria watched with fascination as they eventually positioned themselves by the window.

JC was convinced they had chosen to sit as far away from the counter as possible in the hope that they would go unnoticed and, if an opportunity arose they would no doubt make a discreet exit.

'Aren't you going to serve them, Gloria?' The words were whispered yet, judging by the couple's reaction they had heard every word. The elderly man - seated with his back to JC – arched his back. His whole body seemed to stiffen, much like an agitated feline that was confronting a dangerous adversary. His companion took to mumbling incessantly, vigorously shaking her head on those rare occasions that she drew breath.

'Oh, they can wait!' Gloria's response was audible and said with flagrant contempt. But before JC could formulate a counter argument she turned on her heels and disappeared into one of the little room behind the counter. His first instinct was to pay his bill and depart before she returned but his curiosity got the better of him. He must first see what the elderly couple would do. As he stared expectantly in their direction a slender female figure walked past the café window, briefly looking in his direction she stopped to search furiously in her handbag.

'Oh my God,' he exclaimed. 'It's Maisie!' JC was surprised to see her. He should not have been. He knew she lived nearby and had time on her hands in the mornings, so it made sense that she would wander past his favourite eating establishment from time to time. His first thought was to seek refuge behind the café's oversized menu. There was no way possible that she could have seen him through the tinted window, yet he could not take that chance. Seeing Maisie again resurrected feelings that he thought had been permanently buried. He felt confused and detached from his surroundings. His thoughts were interrupted by the quirky new ring tone on his mobile phone.

'Hello……yes. This is Mr Richards. Human Resources, oh hello. You'd like to offer me the position?! Yes, of course….that's great. Thank you….yes, looking forward to hearing from you soon. Bye..bye.'

JC raised his head from behind the menu to find that Maisie had gone. The elderly couple had also departed. But Gloria had returned, standing patiently with a broad smile on her face in anticipation of what his next words would be.

5

The first day in a new job can be a nervy experience. Particularly if you have not worked for a number of years. It is impossible to recall all the names and faces that are thrown in your direction let alone the location of key offices and meeting rooms. Nevertheless, to someone like JC it is still disappointing to find that you are unable to take the initiative. To utilise your best attributes – his undoubted charm and sense of humour - for fear of committing an elementary faux pas.

It was fortunate then that he was greeted in the lobby by a familiar face, Beatrice McDermott, the Human Resource Manager. Here was someone who, judging from their previous encounter, had already been won over by his charms. But he was surprised by her presence. The role of chaperoning newly appointed staff would not have been part of her remit. Which could mean only one of two things; either she had personal designs on him and was making an early and very public statement of intent or his line manager was more important to the organisation than he realised.

'Hello JC, it's good to see you again. Welcome to Joseph Maitland. I hope… I'm sure you will have a long and prosperous career here at our dynamic, people oriented organisation.'

'It's good to see you too… and thank you.' As they walked towards the elevator he noticed that Beatrice was behaving just as she did on the day of his interview. Gently caressing her hair whenever eye contact was made and laughing out loud for no apparent reason.

'Don't worry JC, I'm not going to bombard you with information. All you will need to know at this moment in time is where the canteen and gentlemen's toilets are. I will then briefly take you to HR where you can meet my team and then we'll finish our tour in Kate's office.'

'Kate?'

'Oh, of course! What a curious development. You have yet to meet Kate. Kate Pritchard, your line manager. Still, you should have received an information pack last week addressing departmental structures and specifically the role you will be performing.'

'Yes of course'.

He hardly glanced at the pack, deciding instead to adopt his usual policy of 'learning on the job'. But the name Kate Pritchard was familiar to him. Perhaps he had absorbed more information then he realised. When they eventually arrived on the 3rd floor – otherwise known as the 'Management Suite'- they stumbled across two more of JC's interviewers, Marvin and Jen, who were embroiled in a heated discussion. Jen must have been grateful for the distraction as she wasted little time in engaging her colleagues.

'Oh hello Beatrice, and er…..Joslin who prefers to be called JC. Am I right?' Joslin nodded.

'Well it is good to see you again JC. Welcome to Joseph Maitland I'm sure....' Beatrice intervened.

'I have already provided him with the customary Joseph Maitland Welcome.'

'Ah, yes' Jen replied snappily,' but not with the same dulcet tones.' There was an uncomfortable silence.

'If you are looking for Kate she is not in her office but I'm sure she wouldn't mind if you both waited in there for her. I on the other hand have to dash. I have a meeting in two... no one minute. I will see you later no doubt Beatrice, JC.......Marvin.'

Up until that moment JC had been convinced that there was an unwritten rule in the City of London which ensured new employees would be exempt from observing disharmony in the work place, for a few weeks at least. Now on his very first day it was evident that his interviewers were continuing where they had left off.

To the naked eye it appeared that Marvin was the sole belligerent but JC refrained from passing judgment, particularly as the warring pair had more in common than he initially suspected. He noticed that they were wearing similar ring bands on their index finger. The words inscribed on them were in Latin but he was unable to determine if they were identical inscriptions.

Beatrice looked uncomfortable the moment she stepped into Kate's office. Less than a minute later she had run out of patience.

'I'm afraid I have to leave JC. I know it's not ideal having to leave you alone in your new manager's office with nothing to do, and on your very first day too but I do have some rather important things to take care of. I'm sure Kate will not be long. This is so unlike her; she knew you were starting this morning and she is rarely late for an appointment.'

'Oh, that's okay Beatrice; I'll be fine. Thank you for your help and for making me feel so welcome.'

Beatrice giggled, caressed her shoulder length hair once again and slowly walked towards the door. Glancing back on two separate occasions before finally leaving.

Kate's office had been completely transformed since his previous visit. There were name plaques on the door and on her desk. Suitably positioned about the room were several photographs of a woman he assumed was Kate and a young girl. There was also a youthful version of the same woman taken in her graduation gown with her arm around the shoulder of an elderly woman. She seemed much happier in this photograph. Ostensibly bathing in the glory of finally achieving her long-term objective. But there was more to it. He sensed a warmth and compassion that had little in common with the cold, detached persona portrayed in the other photographs.

The largest photograph in the room was positioned in the centre of the feature wall, directly behind Kate's desk. In this photograph she was receiving an award from a group of gentlemen wearing identical clothing. Black suits, scarlet shirts and navy blue ties. The photograph appeared to have been taken somewhere in Wrex Tower.

JC could hear the door opening behind him so he rose to his feet so that he could greet his line manager in an appropriate manner.

'Hello Mr Richards and welcome to Wrex Tower. I'm Ms Pritchard.' JC was taken back by her formal greeting.

'Hello Ms Pritchard, I'm delighted to finally meet you.'

'Delighted to finally meet me........are you really?' He had no idea how to respond to her remark.

'Oh, I'm just playing with you JC. I feel it is important that my co-workers can cope with my unique sense of humour, so consider this to be your *baptism of fire* if you like. You do prefer to be called JC do you not?'

'Yes, I do.'

'I knew it, and you can of course address me as Kate.'

His worst fears had been confirmed. The personality of his line manager was all-pervading. Her opening gambit a statement of intent. She will no doubt thrive on calling the shots and playing amusing little games with her expensive new toy. Believing that he will eventually succumb to her irresistible charms. The question now was how would he respond? It was never in doubt. He would respond in the usual way. Keep small talk to a minimum and if placed in an uncomfortable position rely on his sense of humour to save the day.

'Oh, *before we go any further* I have something for you JC.' Kate leaned over her desk, frantically pushing copious sheets of documents to one side.

'I can't seem to find ….. Oh, I noticed you admiring my photographs as I entered the room. I love photographs. They are a constant reminder of how much one has achieved and where one wants to be headed. Did any photo in particular catch your eye?'

'Yes, this one. I assume it is your graduation photo.' Kate's mood immediately changed from chirpy to sombre.

'Yes. Some would say that was a good choice. It is a constant reminder of an 'age of innocence'…my innocence. Refresh my memory JC, did you attend University?'

'Uh, no.'

'Well, for me it was a remarkable experience. I felt alive for the first time. I knew exactly what I wanted and I thought I knew exactly how to get it, but then …...' He desperately hoped she would continue her monologue so that he could gain an insight into what made her tick.

'Time does not change people JC, people change people… Ah, I know where it is.' Kate rifled through her top left hand desk draw and pulled out a gold envelope which had his name embossed on the front. Only then did he notice her ring band. It was remarkably similar to the ones worn by Marvin and Jen.

'This is your invitation to a party on Friday night. It will be held here at Wrex Tower. Well, I say it's an invitation but it is more a directive. New members of staff in particular simply have to attend. Oh, and no spouses allowed I'm afraid.'

JC looked perplexed.

'You should see this as a wonderful opportunity to get to know your new colleagues. So put on your best glad rags.......and do not look so worried JC, you'll love it.'

****

The induction meeting had been running for over an hour and as a consequence JC was finding it increasingly difficult to maintain his concentration levels. It was only when Kate's tone became softer and she utilised expressions such as 'bear with us' and 'unfortunate time restrictions' that he perked up again. He knew from bitter experience that these terminologies rarely benefited junior staff members.

'.....so the logical solution would be for Jen to continue working on these projects as my co-ordinator. She has been heavily involved from the outset and has the trust of our contractors, and in addition we are working to an extremely tight deadline. This means that you will have to *sit it out* for the next few weeks. Take on some of the more..uh... mundane aspects of Jen's role. Take one for the team as it were... and after that things will be exactly as they should be. Any questions?'

Any questions! A number of questions were forming in his mind. But because he was unable to keep up with discussions he dare not raise them for fearing of appearing out of his depth, or dis-interested. As a foretaste of his transitory role he would spend the afternoon partaking in the tasks that PA's dread most of all; filing and photocopying. Kate's offer of an extended lunch break did little to soften the blow but it did provide him with an opportunity to take in a leisurely stroll. He gave Amanda a call to let her know how he was feeling.

'It's not going as well I'd hoped. You can cut the atmosphere with a knife at times.'

'Well, I know that feeling all too well,' she replied coolly. 'That's life I'm afraid and you are just going to have to deal with it.'

'Yes, well on top of that I have to perform clerical duties that are not even related to my manager's objectives and....'

'It's not easy JC. It's never easy. No matter how much it hurts you just have to soldier on.'

It was now apparent why Amanda insisted he called her. He always suspected that she had somehow held him responsible for the decline in her career. Even though she still loved him it did not stop her from gaining solace from his predicament.

He ended the call the best way he knew how without betraying his emotions, but as was often the case after a conversation with Amanda his mood fluctuated wildly. Optimism rose when he foresaw that developments at work could provide invaluable insight into Amanda's tribulations. The catalyst that brings them closer together. But then empathy turned to anger. After all she was not the only one who had made sacrifices in order to achieve their objectives. He had to put his career on hold and abandon his much loved lifestyle to gain credibility in her eyes.

He also severed his relationship with Lenny, which was not an easy thing to do. Particularly as they were still working together at the time. Just like all dependencies the first few weeks apart were the most difficult but it was aided by Lenny's tenuous position at North Sacs International. JC made it seem as though he was doing Lenny a favour when he accepted certain constraints on their friendship. But before long he refrained from attending drinking sessions too, claiming that tiredness - due to the numerous work related courses he was taking - were to blame.

Without JC to mediate between Lenny and Print Room Pete their friendship quickly dissolved. Lenny became isolated at North Sacs and he responded in the only way he knew how; by confronting the source of his distress. His choice of venue however, a lengthy queue at the staff canteen, was a poor choice for such a sensitive matter.

'So JC, I suppose you are unable to make our Friday night session this week or next week either? It's okay you can tell me in advance. I need to know these things in order to keep on top of my busy social calendar.'

'It's not likely Lenny I have so much on at the moment.'

'Yes I know, so you keep saying. It never stopped you in the past from partying. I'll bet it's this new mysterious girlfriend of yours. Is she afraid I will lead you astray?' JC did not respond.

'I never thought I would see the day that a woman would control the great JC! Well if that's the way you are now then maybe its best that you stay in on Friday nights with your pipe and slippers. The ladies in London are safe once again.'

Lenny was becoming increasingly frustrated by JCs refusal to fully engage with him. Without realising what he was doing Lenny continued to raise his voice, thus attracting an increasing number of spectators. An embarrassed JC was finally ready to respond, but not in the way that Lenny had anticipated.

'Well, the ladies have never been in danger with you around. I have never seen you entice a woman, unless it was to aid you in digesting a burger or a kebab after the nightclubs had closed, and after that they were always in a hurry to get away from you.'

The look of anger that Lenny had worn since the encounter began was replaced by one of disbelief.

'Never pulled..... never pulled! What about Bethany?'

'Who?'

'Bethany Wilkins. I was engaged to her for seven weeks. I told you all about her.'

'Yes, but that was before we met. Since then zip, zero, nothing.'

Lenny paused for breath, and as he did so JC watched in fascination as numerous facial expressions took temporary residence on his granite facade. Suddenly and quite unexpectedly a look of intense rage reigned supreme.

'What about Amy?'

'Amy who?'

'Don't tell me that you cannot remember Amy?! Amy was the girl who approached me on the pretence that she liked my Gunners tattoo. While you were chatting up yet another blonde floosy, Amy and I chatted all night long about...well …anything and everything.'

'Oh…..*that* Amy.'

'Yes, that Amy.'

'This is not the place Lenny. Let's talk outside.'

JC lowered his voice as he attempted to shepherd Lenny out of the dining area, but an emotionally charged Lenny was having none of it.

'I am staying right here and talking as loud as I please so that everyone can hear what kind of a friend you really are! Amy and I chatted all night. We…. we even shared a bottle of champagne and spoke of going to concerts and football matches together. Then what happened? Why don't you let everyone know JC?'

'It was a long time ago Lenny.'

'Well not for me, *best* friend. Let me just refresh your memory. You got blown out by the blonde you were with. A rare occurrence, and one that you were not best pleased about. So what did you do? Well, with time quickly running out you decided to sweet talk the nearest available woman. Of course Amy couldn't believe her luck when a handsome bloke like you showed her some attention! You took her from right under my nose, and why? Not because you really liked her but because you could not stand the idea of me leaving the nightclub with a woman on my arm while you went home alone. Thanks friend.'

Exposed by a close acquaintance who had no reason to invent such an anecdote, JC was enraged. Acting purely on instinct he went on the offensive once again.

'You were never going to become an item anyway. When you went off to the bar that night she told me it would be nice if the two of you became good friends. She liked you but that was as far as it went.....clearly she had better taste!'

JC's closing remark put into context what both men had hitherto believed but dare not articulate. That theirs was never an equal relationship. JC was the superior partner, in in every way. And what is more – because of his undisputed good lucks and charisma – he was entitled to be. It was one thing to know your place but deep down they both knew that the subject should never be broached. JC knew that their friendship was irreparably damaged. Even if Lenny could forgive him he could never forgive himself.

The look on Lenny's face mirrored his own. The confusion. The sense of loss. But with a gathering crowd watching intently all JC considered was his own pain and if he was hurting then he wanted Lenny, the instigator of their predicament, to hurt even more. He had not finished yet:

'If I remember correctly Amy ended up coming home with me! I did not have to twist her arm. It was her choice not yours or even mine. Perhaps you should just learn to live with that fact.'

Onlooker's privy to the reputation of Lenny would have been forgiven for believing that his tormentor was in a precarious situation, but as Lenny's enormous frame swayed ominously from side to side there was one person who had no doubt what would happen next. JC could see that Lenny – now utterly humiliated - was in emotional turmoil. A disciple who could still see and communicate with his guru but no longer at a level that made his existence seem tolerable. He was in no condition to cause physical harm to anyone.

'Thanks a lot friend.' Lenny's final words on the matter left JC overwhelmed with grief. He could only watch downhearted as tears trickled down the side of Lenny's face. But there was nothing he could do. The words had been said, and subsequent decisions will be made that would have unforeseen consequences for both men.

6

It was the end of another school day and the children seemed more excited than usual to set eyes on their father as he manoeuvred his way through the throngs of animated grown-ups. Jacob was the first to retain his composure long enough to string a coherent sentence together.

'Can we go Park, daddy?' When the word *park* was mentioned Louise instantly tugged on JC's shirt sleeve, leaving him no alternative but to peer into her unassailable blue eyes. Accorded the full attention of her devoted father she subsequently delivered a more eloquent case for a sojourn until…

'Okay, okay!' he conceded, 'But how would you like to go to a different park for a change. One where they have a special….'

'But daddy,' she anxiously intervened, 'Kim and Lisa said that they were going to *Eden Park.*'

'Yeah,' added Jacob. 'My friend Ricky is going too, and he's got his new Spider-man ball.'

'Well I suppose we can't miss out on seeing Ricky's Spider-Man ball can we? But first, as it's such a hot day how about we grab an ice-cream first and then we can find out the opening times for the new swimming pool.'

'Yeaaah.'

The detour was part of an elaborate ploy to avoid Maisie, the woman who had put him so on edge when she walked passed the café a few weeks ago. On a sunny afternoon like this with normal school hours concluded there was a strong possibility that she would be at the Park with her daughter. Now, half an hour later it was far less likely. Nevertheless the journey to the play area was an uncomfortable one. His feelings of anxiety occasionally lifted by the enthusiastic shouts of the twins, as they greeted friends who they only recently said their good-bye's to at the school gate.

'There's Ricky Daddy! Can I go and play. Pleeease?'

'Wait one minute tiger, you won't be needing your jumper, as it's so hot. Here give it to me.'

'Hello Jacob. Hi Louise.' It was Maisie's voice. That much was unmistakable, and she sounded as chirpy as ever. At the precise moment that she addressed the children JC was in the middle of removing Jacob's jumper, and by the time he had plucked up the courage to look in the direction of her voice she had walked straight by, without breaking stride. He assembled the children:

'Your friends are calling. Why don't you go and play while daddy has a sit down on this bench. You've got half an hour.'

JC was grateful to be alone so that he could process what had just transpired. Maisie was as cordial as ever towards the children, which was a plus, and it was *probably for the best* that she failed to acknowledge his presence. So why did it hurt so much? The ignominy of being ignored by someone he had once flirted with was not a new phenomenon, although admittedly it had been a while.

It occurred to him that his feelings for Maisie could be stronger then he was willing to accept. After all he tended to treat their encounters with the same reverence as his early encounters with Amanda. Recounting the minutest details of their time together to determine if he had responded in the correct manner. It was an experience that often left him feeling emotionally drained.

He still recalls their first meeting with a little unease. It was on a day like any other last summer. He had taken the children to the Park in the afternoon in a bid to expel their excess energies. Louise struck up a friendship with the only other girl in the play area. They were taking it in turns to host imaginary garden tea parties and JC watched with curiosity as the girl's mother became completely absorbed in their pursuit. When her daughter pretended to drop a muffin on the floor and the fruitcake was burnt there was a look of consternation on her face. Conversely when the girls concluded that the tea parties were a huge success she beamed incessantly. She eventually noticed JC furtively observing her every move and, most likely to conceal her embarrassment, engaged him in conversation.

'It's great to see them having so much fun together.'

'Yes it is.' His attempt to muster an equal measure of enthusiasm fell well short of the mark.

'I could never relate to other children when I was their age so I am always delighted to see Sally-Ann making friends.'

'Well, Louise does tend to make friends easily.' JC was instantly aware that his remark was a tad insensitive. He had trivialised what this doting mother understood to be the early signs of a special relationship. She winced, as though physically wounded by his words and when her smile resurfaced it was packaged differently, as though her blinkers had been removed. She still gained pleasure from observing the children but now it was for research purpose only, gauging both the positive and negatives of their collaboration. In a bid to make amends JC decided to initiate a conversation.

'My daughter's name is Louise, but I have already mentioned that....... my son is Jacob and I'm JC.'

'Oh...Hi, yes. It's Sally-Ann...that's my daughter. My name is Maisie.' He chuckled to himself as she said her name. It suited her persona. The way she dressed and styled her hair, the serenity that emanated from her voice and now even her name; it was all synonymous with a bygone age. He surmised that she was heavily influenced by the peace movements of the late sixties. A time when many believed it was possible to change the world by the power of love alone and frowned upon those who chose to acknowledge the paradoxical nature of mankind.

The tone of her voice instantly changed.

'Sally-Ann, we have to go now. Say good-bye to Louise. Good-bye er...JC.'

'Oh, good-bye...Maisie.'

It took Maisie longer than expected to gather her things. An additional length of time was also spent coaxing Sally-Ann away from her new found friend. In the meantime JC tinkered with his mobile phone. He wanted to appear distracted in order to spare them both the discomfort of having to say their good-bye's again. When they were finally ready to leave she held tightly to Sally-Ann's hand and walked quickly towards the park gate. But she paused by the water fountain, less than ten metres from where JC was sitting, and turned to face him. Clearly there was something on her mind.

'We are here most Monday's, Wednesday's and Thursday afternoon's so hopefully the children will get a chance to see each other again soon.... perhaps on Wednesday at around 1.30pm?'

She smiled nervously and without waiting for a response turned to monitor Sally-Ann who had boisterously ran ahead of her. JC was pleased with the outcome. It was nice to part on amicable terms but more importantly he had developed an instant fondness for Maisie. Since the commencement of his relationship with Amanda, JC had decided to trust his instincts when it came to people and he believed that Maisie would make an intriguing acquaintance. She appeared to be open, unassuming and compassionate. All the qualities that he admired in others yet he himself lacked. Who knows, perhaps she would help to make him a better person.

'Come on children I think it's time we went home too. It's getting late and the older children will be coming home from school shortly; no doubt causing chaos in the play area.' Louise happily conceded, seemingly content with her afternoon's performance.

'Can I see Sally-Ann again Daddy?'

'I think so sweetie, very soon.'

'I can't wait to tell mummy that I have a new friend!'

'Well,' JC said quietly but with authority, 'it's probably best not to tell mummy about today. Let's just wait and see how the friendship goes first shall we.' The twins looked at each other with puzzled expressions before turning towards their father and nodding in agreement.

****

It was a quarrel that should never have arisen. JC specifically remembered telling Amanda that the office party was on Friday. He hoped to avoid any confusion because he knew how much she enjoyed catching up with her old University friends on the weekend. Friday evening straight after work being their preferred option.

Their itinerary was always the same. First a little retail therapy before heading for the bars for a drinking session. Amanda always arrived home at a respectable time but she was so energized by the experience that it was impossible for her to sleep. So she would be up until the wee hours of the morning playing music tracks from her university days or getting in touch with relatives in Canada.

'Once again I apologise if I did not make it clear about tonight, but I was told in no uncertain terms that if I do not attend the party I could lose my job. It's as simple as that! It's only one night Amanda, I'm sure Kara and Tabitha will understand.' She did not reply.

'Alternatively they could come over and baby-sit with you. That might be fun! Give them a taste of what it would be like to be a parent.' Amanda was hesitant in her response.

'It's just a real inconvenience because Kara made special arrangements to come down from her Head Office in Watford.'

'Watford? I thought you said that Kara's Head Office was in Woodford? Besides you usually go straight to the venue but today, for some reason you made it all the way home first. So I'm thinking there must have been something there at the back of your mind that set alarm bells ringing about the party. Unless you came home for some other reason?'

'No...No you're right. I think I remember you telling me now. I'm going to have a quick shower. Could you check on the children? Their DVD should be ending round about now.'

He paused for a moment, a little bemused at what had just transpired. As he pondered the salient points of their exchange Amanda's mobile phone vibrated, indicating a text message had been sent. Ordinarily he would have ignored it but on this occasion he thought it might be one of her friends hastily making their way to the rendezvous point, unaware that Amanda was unable to attend. The message was brief:

'Looking forward to tonight.
Hope u r still considering staying over??
All my love
Ray xxx

He stumbled towards the bed, where he sat motionless for some time. The grin on his face was merely a reflex action. On the inside he was inconsolable. Like a man seeing his life flash before his eyes following a near death experience JC vividly recalled key moments of their relationship. The memories were not as clear as in the past. Reminiscent of the inferior quality black and white movies that Amanda adored so much. He could hear the rain splashing against the window pane. It had not rained this heavily for some time.

'It was raining the day we first met. Huh…. the perfect couple. My God!'

A vigorous shake of the head was followed by composed steps towards the full length free standing mirror. It had recently been repositioned between the bedside table and the window. He could not bear to go through his usual grooming ritual. Instead he peered directly into his own eyes – the windows of his soul - as if searching for answers that were apparent to everyone save himself.

'You were right Lenny, 'Don Juan' has definitely lost his Mojo.' Although bitterly upset he was determined to respond in a rational manner and that meant going to the party. It was vital that he remained in employment; kept his newly gained financial independence. There could be a harmless explanation for the intimate wording of Ray's text but a frank discussion now could leave him mentally unprepared for the evening's undertakings. He could hear the shower being switched off and a gentle thud as Amanda stepped out of the shower. She was returning to the bedroom.

'You are not still preening yourself, are you? I bet you haven't even checked on the children. That's not like you at all.'

'No, I haven't' he replied calmly, 'I'll do so on the way out. Got to go.'

'Okay have fun.'

****

JC took a mini-cab to the venue. To avoid engaging in conversation with the driver he placed his headphones over his ears and attached it to his iPhone, but no music was played. He sought only to peer sombrely through the car window and observe the cumbersome drops of rain as they lazily merged to form mighty rivulets. He had changed considerably in the last few years. Not as exciting or spontaneous as he used to be.

80

Amanda saw these changes as a negative, but additional responsibilities required him to develop as a person.

While his relationship with Amanda had become turbulent he was finding that a different type of woman was becoming attracted to him. The *yummy mummies* were in awe of fathers who were conversant with all aspects of child rearing. He recalled eavesdropping on Maisie in the park one day as she spoke to another woman about her ideal man:

> 'I do not miss Sally-Ann's father. In fact I was quite relieved when he told me that he needed time to consider his parental responsibilities. I decided to give him all the time he needed by leaving Nottingham as soon as I could and move to London.
>
> Looks are important but they are not the be all and end all. An ideal partner has to be able to make me feel at ease when we are together. He has to be practical, caring, especially to children, loyal, funny… well make me laugh for sure. But just as important is to have someone that I can talk to for hours about anything and everything and then still want to talk some more. That is the real test of a relationship.'

At the time those words were spoken Maisie, JC and their respective children had been meeting regularly on weekday afternoons. The bond that developed between the children, and particularly Louise and Sally-Ann surpassed even Maisie's expectations. Their excursions took in libraries, café's, the local swimming baths and on one occasion a trip to the cinema. JC enjoyed being part of an extended collective and found himself inadvertently treating his relationship with Maisie as a surrogate for the emotional void that existed in his life.

The end of the summer heralded the beginning of the new school year, and all three children were to attend primary school for the first time. Sally-Ann was accepted into a local Catholic School while Jacob and Louise were enrolled at a reputable state school. They had been so close for so long but now there was no valid reason for them to assemble as they had done before.

Broaching the subject was never an option for JC as it might be interpreted as an attempt to take their relationship to another level. It was Maisie who broke the impasse:

'So JC what are you going to do with yourself now that the children will not be around?'

'I will look for a job eventually, but first I am going to enjoy myself for a few weeks.'

'Yes, me too, though I will be at a bit of a loose end until then...I...well...' Maisie's coyness never ceased to bring a smile to his face, but it was her eagerness to talk openly and honestly regardless of how she was feeling inside that most impressed him. On this occasion he decided to give her a helping hand.

'If you were about to suggest that we should meet up on Monday afternoon at the usual time then I am all for it, but we'd better not meet up here. It might seem a bit strange if two adults turned up in the children's play area without any children! Where do you suggest we meet?'

'Ah, well there is a curious looking Café called the Raison D'etre which is located not far from the high street. I have always been tempted to go in there but not on my own…...but if you'd rather not.'

'No, that's fine. I only hesitated because I have been there before. It's hardly the most salubrious place in the world but if you are curious about going then sure, let's do it.'

A rendezvous without the children present could be construed as a date, but JC was able to justify his decision in a number of ways. Firstly, Maisie was aware that he had a partner. Louise and Jacob often referred to *mummy* and their home life. Secondly he was not doing anything that he did not normally do. They were in the habit of meeting up on Monday afternoons and the fact that the children would not be present was immaterial. Finally and most importantly of all he enjoyed the status quo. His meetings with Maisie never failed to transport him to a happier place where no emotional demands were made on him, he felt at ease talking about everything except intimacy, and that was how he wanted their relationship to continue.

It came as no surprise to him that Maisie arrived late; she was always late. What did surprise him was the behaviour of the Café waitress. As soon as Maisie sat at his table, an anxious expression appeared on her face. She immediately scuttled into the back room, failing to re-appear over ten minutes later. JC could no longer hide his frustration.

'I hope it wasn't something I said.'

'You hope what wasn't something you said?'

'Oh no. It's just that Nadia, the waitress hasn't returned and I was just wondering where she was.'

'Nadia? You didn't say you were a regular.'

'Well, I'm not really. It's just that I'm good friends with the manager, Gloria. Speaking of which she is usually here by now, you will like her.' Maisie sighed.

'Look JC, I am dying for a cuppa and we don't have a great deal of time. We could go back to mine. It's only ten minutes from here and on the way we can pick up some biscuits at a local shop.'

****

JC looked like a man heading for the gallows as he ascended the stairs leading to Maisie's front porch. On entering the property they were met by a cacophony of odours that emanated from a variety of sources, the most dominate being the exceedingly pungent pair of sneakers that were poorly hidden behind the huge pot plant in the lobby. JC noted that all the ground floor rooms were fitted with locks that required a key for access. It was a shared dwelling, with paying tenants occupying each room. They rarely touched on the subject of finances but JC had always assumed that Maisie was of middle class background with a relatively comfortable lifestyle.

'I'm on the first floor. There's a Kitchen next door to our room so hopefully we will be able to have a cup of coffee in peace. I'm afraid some of the tenants are not the nicest of people.'

He nodded and smiled. Maisie returned his smile with an affectionate expression that both enthused and concerned him in equal measures.

The coffee was consumed without interference from the other occupants and JC found himself beginning to enjoy the experience. But he was also wary of the time. He did not want to be late to collect the children from school on their first day.

'Before you go JC, Sally-Ann has been saying for some time now that she would like to give Louise a few of her toys. Come with me and I'll get them out for you.'

Maisie feebly attempted to push her room door open before blushing with embarrassment when she realised that she had forgotten to use her key. Once inside she immediately scanned through a huge collection of toys that were forcing their way out of a wooden toy box. JC watched with fascination. He had known her for just a few months yet her movement, the way she sighed with exasperation when she could not find what she was looking for and the cute expression on her face when she realized it had fallen behind Sally-Ann's bed. It all seemed more than just familiar. It was as though she had been an integral part of his life for a considerable time.

'Sorry JC, I'll give you the one outstanding toy when we next meet.'

'It's really no problem. Louise would not have been expecting anything anyway so she will be delighted with what she has got.'

They stood in silence, staring into each other's eyes before simultaneously bursting into fits of laugher. It was Maisie who irrevocably changed the mood by saying something quite unexpected.

'I think you are wonderful JC. You probably heard what I said in the park the other day about my ideal man, well you are all those things and more.'

Without warning Maisie placed her arms around his shoulders and kissed him passionately. As they remained entwined he glanced over her shoulder and noticed for the first time the squalid conditions of her room. Books and items of clothes were scattered in all directions. Unopened official looking letters lay on the floor. A plate full of food with spaghetti strands dangling over the side was precariously placed on a rickety stool.

Maisie's lips were still pressed firmly against his but now her eyes were closed and her embrace more passionate; compensating for his inability to reciprocate. But whatever she did it could not change the fact this was not how it was meant to be. Since establishing a relationship with Amanda, JC had resisted numerous opportunities to form intimate relationships. He still craved the attention but would tactfully withdraw before physical contact was made. It made him feel even closer to Amanda, as it proved how committed he was to their relationship. Now. Now he felt disgusted with himself. He could no longer deny his feelings for Maisie but by the same token he could not succumb to his desires. He was not for having sordid little affairs with besotted women whenever the mood takes him; at least not anymore.

'I have to go Maisie…..I just have to go.' The look on Maisie's face was one of utter dismay; from her perspective she had just bared her soul to a man who, according to all the signals would reciprocate. She felt confused and humiliated, but before she had time to collect her thoughts and respond he was gone.

'I could not do it to you Amanda,' He whispered to himself in the mini-cab. 'No matter what problems we were having. I could not do it to you.'

'Are you okay back there mate? We're about to arrive.' The cab driver's caustic tones brought him back to the present. Lost in thought the journey had taken no time at all. The time for reflecting was over. It was time for the party to begin.

7

The evening progressed in a manner he had not envisaged. Straitlaced managers who made an art form of treating their subordinates with disdain were pivotal to the vibrant all-embracing spectacle that was unfolding before his eyes. Natural inclinations that had been adroitly curtailed even under the most intense conditions readily succumbed to the combined sway of the pulsating dance music and the spectacular LED lighting. The latter unquestionably enhancing the sensual movements of established and newly formed couples alike. The atmosphere was abetted by the unrestricted distribution of fine quality champagne from the 'open bar' and singing waiters serving a variety of sweetmeats.

In fact the waiters were the unsung luminaries of the evening. Their capacity to swiftly assemble when a sufficient number of new guests had arrived and perform dance routines to popular noughties dance tracks even managed to rouse JC from his state of contemplation. But when the performance had ended and the element of surprise extinguished thoughts of Amanda and her mysterious acquaintance once again governed his thoughts.

Like intuitive animals sensing a recalcitrant interloper his fellow party revellers were eager to keep their distance. All save one. A nervy looking woman standing alone at the far end of the makeshift bar finally mustered the courage to approach him.

'Well JC, it seems as if you and I are the only ones not having fun.'

'Appearances can be deceiving' he replied. 'I'm actually having a great time. But I'm afraid you have me at a disadvantage. I usually never forget a name, especially that of a beautiful woman, but I have been introduced to so many people this week.'

'I see.........' she replied coolly. A look of disappointment etched on her face.

'...I see you haven't changed a bit. Still chatting up any woman in a skirt or is it still just the blondes you go for? Of course I wasn't a blonde back then.'

He could not say what was more disturbing. The fact that he had pitifully flirted with someone he had discarded in the past or that he was unable to recollect the encounter. The woman who stood before him was slim and relatively young, most likely in her mid to late twenties. The illusion that they were of similar height was bolstered by her unique dress sense; notably black stilettoes and an elegant tight-fitting Edwardian style blue evening dress. The latter carelessly draped over her slender shoulder, giving the distinct impression that she had consumed more alcohol then was actually the case. He was captivated by her classic good looks and wholesome countenance, which seemed somewhat out of place in the extant hedonistic environment. Surely he would have remembered being intimate with such a unique individual.

'Well JC, I suppose I should apologise for gawping at you but I was trying to pluck up the courage to come over and offer my condolence for the loss of your dear friend. I know it was some time ago now but it must have come as a shock to you. It certainly did to me.'

'My Fr.....Amy... you're Amy! Oh my goodness. So you've dispensed with the Goth look. I'm sorry, I didn't ...what are you doing here?!'

'I work here. In marketing on the fifth floor. I have been working here for the last eight years; since leaving college. I did tell you where I was working the night we...we.....'

'Ah, yes I'm sure you did, but in my defence it was a long time ago. How did you hear of his death?'

'I kept ringing him and sent several texts but there was no response, so...it was me who contacted the authorities.'

'You?!....... He never told me you had stayed in touch.'

'I know....and how could he? He would have been totally humiliated if you had found out he was in contact with the girl that *you* had stolen from him.'

'It was not like that and you know it.'

'No. Then what was it like JC, please tell me?'

He was too emotionally drained to defend the indefensible. Amy continued:

'On the night we met I had given Lenny my telephone number long before we left him standing alone in the nightclub. Obviously I did not expect to hear from him again. But he rang about a week later; no doubt after he realised that you had no intention of calling me. I suppose we both knew from the start that we had a lot in common. Once we got over the initial awkwardness we became good friends. Did you know he convinced himself that you did it for his own good? He considered it to be a wake-up call. You know, a reminder that intimate relationships would never work out for him.'

'It sounds as if you grew to care for him deeply?' Amy sighed.

'He never considered intimacy between us to be an option after that first night, and I was just glad to be a part of his life. But he never really got over the break-up of your friendship. No matter what I tried to do there was always a void in his life that could never be filled.'

'Je suis désolé' he said softly. 'I mean I'm truly sorry for how I used to be.'

'Huh! I know what it means JC, but speaking in French? I thought you only did that when you were stressed out by Lenny. Even now he seems to be having an effect on you.'

Lenny had obviously spoken to Amy at great lengths on the depth of their friendship, but he wondered if she truly knew what was going through his mind during those last fateful days. JC knew all too well. Exactly one week after Lenny had passed away JC received a phone call from Ernest & Sons Solicitors, urging him to pay them a visit. Lenny had bequeathed a large suitcase to JC which contained a number of items. Memorabilia of their times together.

Hidden amongst the nightclub ticket stubs, encyclopaedia's and collection of limited edition marvel comics was an envelope addressed to JC. There was a letter inside. The handwriting was shaky and on a downward curve, which led JC to surmise that it was written not long before his passing. It read:

Hi JC,

Here's to you old friend. I still call you friend because that is the way I will always remember you. I couldn't believe it when we first started hanging out together. That someone like you, cool, handsome, funny and intelligent would want to hang out with an overweight, lumbering idiot like me, yet we had some great times. It was not only the partying that was brilliant but also just talking about all kind of things, and sometimes not even talking was okay. Just knowing that I meant something to you would get me through the day.

I think I knew from the start that being close to someone as well loved as you would be painful for someone like me. There would always be another conquest and our friendship would become a little shaky for a while, but that was okay. In many ways it made our friendship even more exciting. Everything was great until that bitch came along! The hatred that I feel for her cannot be described, but you love her and if you love her then she must have some redeeming qualities. I just find it impossible to live without my best pal anymore, but I do not think of this as good-bye but more of a see you later. Because if we can't be together in this world then I am hoping we will be together in the next.

Until we meet again.

Lenny

Lenny and Amanda had never met. JC went to great lengths to see to that, but he often wondered what would have happened if they had. If Lenny had been able to talk his way out of working late on the night of his first encounter with Amanda, then the relationship would probably not have developed. Lenny would have been alert to the unique rapport between them and resorted to underhand tactics, designed to ensure that Amanda would never want to speak to either of them again. Lenny's parting letter all but confirmed as much. JC was convinced he made the correct decision then and he was about to make another now, by ensuring that Amy would never know of Lenny's final thoughts. It would no doubt tarnish the wonderful memories that she had of him.

I wouldn't have thought this party was your kind of thing, Amy.' A wry smile immediately appeared on her face, indicating she was satisfied with his analysis.

'To be totally honest it is even more surprising that I received an invitation at all. I have never been asked to mingle with the *in crowd* before.

Well, I suppose I hardly fall into the high-flier category...' She hesitated for a moment.

'...but there are times when what I think or feel is irrelevant. When Kate Pritchard personally hands you an invite it would be unwise to turn her down. She is not the type of person you say no to.'

'Now why does that not surprise me?'

'Oh, you've met her.'

'Every day this week. I'm her new PA slash office manager.' There was a moment's silence.

'Oh....Oh! I heard that she had employed some new tottie....er no offence JC, but I had no idea it was you. This is becoming very... intriguing.'

The tone of her voice sent a shiver down his spine. Amy was now deep in thought. Her body language visibly changed, which led him to believe that she had no intention of revealing what was on her mind. Conversely JC believed that Amy was easy to read. Fundamentally good natured; passionate and with high moral values so there was a distinct possibility that he could manipulate her into providing the information he so desperately wanted.

'If you are concerned about me then don't be. I have handled far tougher bosses then Kate in the past.'

'Really! The fact you have just made that statement tells me that you have no idea what she is capable of.'

'Well now,' he hastily replied, 'I too was a little bit concerned to begin with, but after a frank discussion about my role she has been nothing but professional, plus I have become good friends with key members of staff in Human Resource. The first sign of inappropriate behaviour and I will have her up on harassment. She may appear to be as hard as nails but underneath she's just a pussycat.'

A look of astonishment emerged on Amy's face. She scoured the room, ostensibly concerned that Kate or her cohorts might be in the vicinity. Finally reassured she drew breath before moving closer to him.

'Kate Pritchard sat at my table in the staff canteen oh... roughly seven years ago. It was the first time she had made an effort to talk to me. She was not as high up in the organisation as she is now but she was already commanding a good deal of respect. We talked mainly about my career prospects and social life; nothing unusual at first. I got a little concerned though when she started asking me about my personal life and who I was dating, was it serious and am I going to see them again.' JC smiled.

'Ah well, thank you for the trip down memory lane but I can't see what any of this has to do with me.'

'Okay, well how about this to be getting on with. The night before was the first and only time that we slept together and the first time that I had been intimate with someone for over a year. You have to admit it is highly coincidental that I was being questioned on that particular day. At first I thought she was gay and had a thing for me. You know....perhaps she was stalking me, saw us together and became jealous enough to finally make her move, but since then she has not so much as glanced in my direction until……'

'Until this party invite?'

'Well, I'm no Sherlock Holmes but I think I can safely say that once again everything revolves around you, Mr Richards.'

He continued to stare at Amy in the vein hope that she had a rational explanation for Kate's conduct. But Amy was no longer willing to engage in conversation. Someone else was now in her line of vision and fast approaching, and by the startled look on her face he knew it could only be one person.

'Ah, my two favourite people engrossed in conversation, and from the look on your faces it appears to be very interesting indeed.' She turned to face Amy.

'Oh do tell?' Kate announced her arrival in typical fashion, by putting her prey on the spot. But JC was exceptional at putting people at ease and on this occasion he realised that he had to buy Amy some time to regain her composure.

'Why don't we save the long-winded discussion for another time and head on to the dance floor? I haven't had a dance all night and it would give my reputation a boost if I was spotted dancing with the two most beautiful women at the party.' Kate somehow managed to refrain from grinning with satisfaction.

'I think you are being somewhat elusive JC. I do hope we can have that discussion at a later date but for now how can I possibly turn down an offer like that. Are you coming uh…Amy.'

'No thank you Kate, unfortunately my dress was not made for dancing in. I think I'll have a sit down.'

Once on the dance floor Kate wasted little time in asking probing questions on JC's hopes and ambitions. He enjoyed being the centre of attention. It was proving to be a welcome distraction from his personal problems. That is until Kate's line of questioning turned to his relationship with Amanda.

'Has the fact that she is no longer a high profile celebrity impacted on your relationship?'

'Well, she was hardly that, but no….not at all.'

'Well, for a while there she was hardly out of the newspapers. You too if I remember correctly. If she wasn't presenting the weather forecast she was on a reality TV show or selling her life story to a celebrity magazine. Then there were the fast cars and eating out at the finest restaurants. I suppose having children must have had a big impact? It must have hit you both so hard….. I imagine you to be someone who enjoyed being in the public eye?'

'I can take it or leave it.'

'And Amanda. How did she take it?'

'Likewise.' She paused for a moment.

'I am happy that you have found your ideal partner JC.' He relaxed his guard a little and smiled.

'But if you are so perfect together then why are you not married? Granted you appear to be a bit of a philanderer but I see you as the type of man that...well, once you have found the right women, you would be more than happy to put a ring on her finger. The whole white wedding thing.'

JC's cool façade, seemingly impenetrable mere moments ago was being clinically dismantled by Kate. Unable to take much more of her assault he turned to walk away. But before he could do so she reached out and grabbed his arm.

'Look I'm sorry for my comments. They were merely observations. It is apparent that something is wrong with you and I am concerned that it might eventually have a negative effect on not just JC the employee but also JC the man. Now to totally change the subject do you want to see something really cool?'

Without waiting for a response Kate took his hand and led him through the throngs of dancing employees. Their journey ended at the far end of the corridor, where the defective elevator was located.

'Uh, Kate we can't go in there. It's not safe.'

'Appearances can be deceiving. I'll tell you a remarkable statistic JC. Did you know that this elevator has had an *out of order* sign attached to it for over five years and no-one has ever asked why it has taken so long to repair? No-one! I know because I check with office services at least once a week. If one of our employees actually had the balls to pose the question then I just might have to tell them the truth.' She moved closer to whisper in his ear.

'It has never truly been out of use, at least not for a select few.'

'Select?' His curiosity had been aroused. 'I have noticed some senior managers wearing Latin inscribed rings; you included. And the photo in your office. Those men dressed in identical clothes. Are you Freemasons?'

'Uhm, how observant of you. Yes, I suppose we are of sorts.'

'And you want me to join?'

She smiled intently before pressing the elevator buttons in sequence, as one would enter their pin number at a cash dispenser. The doors opened to reveal a quaint mini-bar suitably positioned on a red and white striped woven rug. Resting on top of the mini-bar was a bottle of champagne and one champagne glass. The walls and ceiling were comprised of glass panels, adding to the feeling of space and more ominously, that they were not alone. After signalling JC to enter Kate chuckled in a surprisingly husky tone.

'Oh, JC it's not a question of enrolling. It's more a question of experiencing the delights that are on offer before deciding whether or not it is for you.'

He was unconvinced by Kate's rhetoric. Her facial expression was a far more accurate barometer of her intent and on this occasion it led him to believe that this was an all or nothing offer. He was in the grip of a dilemma. There were limits to what he would do to keep his job, but without knowing what was required of him how was he to know if those limits would be reached? He eagerly accepted the champagne and on doing so caught a glimpse of himself in one of the glass panels. Although still well-groomed he looked tired, his eyes glazed. His nose appeared elongated to the extent that it now resembled his father's. Hitherto when observing his reflection he saw only the salient features of his mother, her round shape face, penetrating blue eyes, the curves of her lips. The thought of acquiring his father's traits as time went by made him shudder. But perhaps that was how it was meant to be from here on in. The years of trading in on his boyish good looks had passed and the era of a harsher, manly façade had dawned. He would now look in the mirror and be constantly reminded of all the hearts he had broken. The friends he had treated with disrespect. The colleagues he had manipulated in order to get on in life. Until one day the transformation would be complete. All that would be left is a man, yes but a sad and lonely man who would bare an uncanny resemblance to the people he would rather not to be reminded of.

He glanced over at Kate and wondered how old she was. Possibly five, ten years his senior and still very attractive. Now it was mainly women of Kate's age, who were either divorced, separated or considering having affairs with a younger man who were providing him with a backward glance. Kate was offering him something - he did not know what - but how long will it be before women such as Kate lose interest. Amanda was enjoying her life. He owed it to himself to live the lifestyle that he once thrived on for as long as he could.

'We have almost reached the basement.'

Her words were hurried, as though she was consumed with excitement or perhaps anxiety, he could not tell which.

'I didn't know this building had a basement.'

'It can only be accessed by using this elevator. Very few have seen what you are about to see. The real fun is about to begin. Are you in?'

Without hesitation he picked up the champagne glass and consumed the remainder of its contents.

'Yes,' He said confidently. 'I'm most definitely in.'

The elevator door opened to reveal a hive of activity. Men and women of all shapes and sizes wearing full length gowns were working tireless, ostensibly for a common cause.

'Wow, so this must be the masonic lodge?'

Kate did not reply. It did not matter. In truth it was self-explanatory. The solemn atmosphere and ornate furnishings spoke volumes and less than 10 metres to his left was a large imposing door. It was where the activity was at its peak. He deduced that it must be the inner sanctum.

It was apparent that something out of the ordinary was about to happen. He was about to question Kate on the significance of their conduct when he was distracted by a strange grey mist. It appeared from nowhere and was engulfing the whole basement. Why did no-one else show concern? And why was no-one else suffering from adverse effects? Feeling light headed and unsteady on their feet? In a vain attempt to gather his thoughts JC closed his eyes and vigorously shook his head. When he opened his eyes Kate was nowhere to be seen. Instead there was another woman standing in front of him. She took him by the hand and led him through the large door. JC wanted to explain to her exactly how he was feeling but the words would not leave his lips. Only then did he realise that no-one else was affected by the mist because there was no mist. He alone must have been drugged and the symptoms he was having were the side-effects of that drug. It was most likely added to the glass of champagne that Kate was so eager to dispense.

Now came the hallucinations. An oak tree that was made of ice or was it glass? It had branches but no leaves. It began to shimmer and it seemed to be calling out to him. He wanted to reach out and touch it but feared the consequences. The woman now led him to an altar. She spoke softly, uttering the same words over and over again. Eventually he realised she was saying just one word; *sleep*. He had no option but to comply.

Part Two

Crossing the Bridge

8

The glare of the sun was barely palpable through the exceptionally dense red curtains. Having lost all track of time he was too exhausted to raise his head from the pillow. All he could do was close his eyes once more and hope that the pounding headache and nausea would soon dissipate. He did not remember drinking excessively. In fact he could not remember much at all. After several minutes of trying to *sleep it off* one final concerted effort was made to get out of bed.

'Okay after three....one, two, three...uh!' He was upright. One rapid movement later and he was perched precariously on the edge of the bed, fingers digging desperately into the mattress for support. Although still laying claim to the aforementioned symptoms he could at least visually interpret his poorly lit surroundings. In his immediate line of vision he could see a worn leather armchair, accessorized by a *Rupert the Bear* embossed cushion. The latter only recently puffed out so that it would look at its best. The armchair appeared ill at ease with the pink and green striped wallpaper and a landscape painting dominated by horses in a field.

There was a loud knock on the door quickly followed by the sound of an irate female voice that could not fail to command the attention of anybody within hearing range.

'Can you open the door, Joslin?'

Ailments all but forgotten he quickly sprung to his feet in order to obey her command. In she walked, tall and elegant, even in her nightgown. She was carrying a heavily laden tray. Disappointingly, her features were concealed by her face pack.

'I thought I'd bring you breakfast in bed, but unfortunately I had to get you out of bed to bring it to you.'

He politely laughed at her attempt at humour and sat back on the bed so that his torso was fully supported by the headboard.

'You must be my other half?' he said dryly.

'Oh very amusing, I'll have you know that once I take this muck off of my face you will hardly recognise me'.

'And that's a good thing is it?'

Her attempt to chortle at his riposte was stifled by the weight of the face pack. His eyes diligently pursued her as she carefully placed the tray onto the bedside table and walked a little nervously towards the bedroom door. Before leaving she turned and stared back at him. Piercing green eyes were her only identifiable trait yet their effect on him was bordering on hypnotic. He was intrigued by the way they imposed themselves on her temporary coffee-coloured façade & absurdly wondered if they had actually burrowed their way through the face pack to independently create the eye slits.

'You seem a little shaky Joslin. You clearly had one too many last night. Greg promised me he would make sure you behaved yourself but I knew he couldn't be trusted.'

'Yes, that's probably it' he replied. 'Perhaps I'll just rest for a little bit longer.' Her voice became stern once again.

'Rest! Wouldn't it be wonderful if we could all have a rest whenever we wanted too?' She moved swiftly towards the bay windows and pulled back the curtains.

'Some natural light and fresh air might do you some good then straight after breakfast the pigs will need feeding.' This time she moved confidently towards the bedroom door. Still desperately wanting to speak with her Joslin leaned forward to call out her name, before realising that he could not remember what it was!

'Er... sweetie.'

'Sweetie! That's a bit romantic for you isn't it? It's always Suzy or Suze.' She seemed to be expecting a witty retort, but when none was forthcoming an uncomfortable silence ensued.

'I'll see you downstairs. Don't forget downstairs in 20 minutes as the pigs will need feeding.' She closed the door behind her.

'The pigs!' The odorous smell that immediately pervaded the room once the window had been opened. The smell of the farmyard still surprised him with its potency.

'You'd think I'd be used to the smell by now. Goodness! How could I not even remember her name?' Ohhh, that Greg has a lot to answer for.'

****

Joslin hurriedly ate his breakfast and was ready for work within the allotted time frame. Suzy was waiting for him by the back door. She was dressed in appropriate daytime attire but her face pack was still in place.

'Don't forget your list of chores on the kitchen table. I'll have your lunch ready at twelve fifteen, but don't worry I'll give you a shout as usual. Come on, off you go now.'

Joslin was surprised by the ease in which he applied himself that morning. The hangover now a thing of the past, he found that the only restriction to his exceptional work rate was the intensity of the blazing sun. His work methods were appreciated by the livestock as they responded in a manner that indicated they were accustomed to his adept handling. Joslin's temperament contrasted favourably with his mood earlier that morning. His conversation with Suzy had left a bitter taste in his mouth but he acknowledged that she had every right to be aggrieved. If he drank too much then that was his decision. He should not expect to be rewarded with a lie-in for his efforts.

Instinctively he grabbed hold of his left hand and fiddled with his wedding ring.

'Suze is a feisty one alright, but at least when the war paint comes off she will look a lot more like the woman I married.' His chuckling was abruptly halted by Suzy's bellowing voice, which contemptuously surmounted the melodious chirping of passing swallows.

'Joslin, lunch is ready.'

'Yep, coming.' From his vantage point less than a metre from the barn he was able to identify the elegant outline of her body as she waited patiently by the kitchen door. The face pack had been removed and judging from the sound of her voice and the lingering wave she too was in a better mood than she had been that morning.

The ground became firmer underfoot as he neared the farmhouse so he intentionally dragged his feet to loosen the mud that was wedged to his boots. As he came within a metre of the farmhouse he noticed a distinct change in Suzy's demeanour. She had taken up an unnatural pose, as though preparing to have her photo taken. Her apathetic expression contributed to the impression that she was waiting for someone else. Someone of far more importance. He took this to mean that she wanted to be complimented on her appearance. Evidently a lot of effort had been made on his behalf so he did not wish to disappoint.

He observed long enough to convince her that an extensive inspection had been made, but when it came to providing feedback he was lost for words. Suzy looked absolutely stunning! To his surprise the words of his father sprung to mind:

'No matter how long or how much you love someone you will one day, and for some unknown reason suddenly see them in a different light. If you like what you see then that's fine. You are a lucky man. If you do not like what you see then it's time to move on. No-one can reverse time, so it is unlikely that they will ever fill your heart with unbridled joy again.'

His father was openly discussing past conquests with some men he had met in the local Barbers shop. Joslin was sitting proudly by his side. Just thirteen years of age. A young lad waiting patiently to get his hair cut, and hoping to hear some words of wisdom from someone he considered to be the wisest of men.

The comment made no sense to him at all back then but now it was all too clear. On a purely physical level Suzy was flawless. A more perfect body could not have been formed. Each time he addressed her flawless features he seemed to notice something different, the curvature of her nose or the shape of her eyes that made her appear even lovelier. He was indeed *a lucky man*. She had changed her outfit again. This time wearing a predominately white figure hugging pastoral dress and fashionable lace up shoe boots, impracticable for life on the farm but on this day it had admirably served its purpose.

'Yes, I still like what I see.'

'Er…well if that's the highest praise I am going to receive I'll just have to accept it.'

'I'm sorry Suzy….it's just that you look so amazing. You took me completely by surprise.'

'Better; keep going.'

'I see you're wearing contact lenses'

'What?'

'Contact lenses. Your eye colour has changed from green to blue.'

'Oh yes do you like them?'

'Yes, you…everything looks wonderful.' His words had the required effect. But as Suzy smiled contentedly Joslin found himself overwhelmed by a myriad of emotions; pride, passion, contentment. All the emotions one might expect to feel when your wife had made the effort to look as beautiful as the day you first met. Conversely, one unsolicited emotion remained dormant from the moment he had shaken off the effects of his hangover. A terrible sense of loss, but for whom or what he could not say.

****

Suzy's desire to spice up their day continued into the evening when Joslin was treated to his favourite meal for supper. Roast beef and Yorkshire pudding, followed by apple crumble and custard. They then retired to the drawing room where Joslin wasted no time in making himself comfortable on the sofa. The mood of the evening seemed set when they casually shared a bottle of chardonnay and listened to jazz music on the radio.

'Ah Suze, I am absolutely exhausted! It's remarkable to think I that I have been working to this level of intensity, day in and day out for years.' She smiled and looked at him intently. He could see only love in her eyes.

'You are my hero Joslin, you always have been and you always will be.' Suzy walked tentatively towards him. Once seated she gently rested her head on his shoulder. This act alone was enough to inspire her to broach subjects of a more serious nature. She spoke of extending the farmhouse and increasing the range of produce that they sold at the local market. Each time she made a suggestion it would be followed by an anxious wait for a response. As though it was imperative that an immediate consensus was reached. Too tired to enter into discourse he would grunt his approval, which merely encouraged her to resume with more gusto.

As the evening wore on and the wine took effect Suzy nestled her head firmly into his chest, murmuring sounds of contentment and as she did so it seemed inconceivable that she could be any happier. Joslin however was beginning to feel a little overwhelmed.

'I don't like jazz music.'

'Okay' she said calmly.'

'I'll change the radio station. Now stop trying to change the subject and *tell me what you think*?'

'About what?'

'Have you not been listening to a word I said?!' Joslin sat up sharply. Forcing Suzy to relinquish her comfortable position.

'I'm sorry sweet…I mean Suze I'm just…'

'A little tired? I know, and here I am rattling on.'

'No it's fine. Look Suze, I've never really liked being called Joslin. It's not because my father named me. It just sounds so …. cold. Perhaps you could call me by my middle name. Yeah, Chris isn't too bad, or perhaps Jos or even just J for short?'

He could feel Suzy's willowy frame stiffen against his body; she drew breath before responding:

'I love the name Joslin. It suits you to a tee. It's a strong, uncommon name. Why on earth would you want to abbreviate your name?'

Suzy's aggressive tone took him by surprise. He needed a moment to compose himself before replying. But within that short time frame her calm, compliant exterior had returned.

'I'm sorry Joslin that was totally out of order. I just wanted today to be perfect and….. I love you just the way you are, but if you want me to call you something a little…. cuddlier than I will. Just give me a day or two to think of something.' Suzy sprang to her feet, stretched out her arms and yawned unconvincingly.

'I think I will call it a night but you can stay up and finish that second bottle of wine if you want.'

'Okay Suze. I'm sorry if I upset you too. I didn't realize how important it was to you.'

Suzy smiled and turned towards the drawing room door.

'Just one more thing Suzy.' He heard her sigh before turning to face him. He was aware that her meticulously planned evening had been ruined, and to make matters worse she was as much to blame for it as him. He also knew that all she wanted to do right now was to be tucked up in bed, perhaps to muse over what she could do to make tomorrow a better day. Yes, Joslin appreciated all of that but he had one question that needed to be answered before the night was over, otherwise he would not get a wink of sleep.

'Suzy I…'

'What is it Joslin?' She said softly. 'Why do you have such a worried look on your face?'

'Well, it's just…I was wondering…..where are the children?

9

How long had it been? Seconds? Minutes perhaps? He could not say. Joslin's world seemed to turn on its head just as Suzy was revealing her amorous intentions for the evening. Inexplicably his mood changed. He impudently announced his dislike of jazz music. Then he expressed his dislike of his Christian name, hoping that together they could come up with a palatable alternative. Yet somehow he was made to feel guilty for even broaching the subject. Uncomfortable with the direction their conversation was heading Suzy decided to retire for the evening, leaving him with extensive pent-up emotions. Why these feelings had manifested at that particular moment in time was unclear to him, but he could not leave things as they were.

There was now an awkward silence to add to the tension that had been building ever since the question was posed. The longer it was taking her to respond the more accepting he became of the absurdity of his remark. It just did not make sense. The usual paraphernalia associated with family life was nowhere to be seen. There were no photographs of children taking pride of place on the mantelpiece, nor were their toys of any description lying around; not even in those annoying, awkward to reach nook and crannies. The house was kept in immaculate condition, and yet he had a paternal yearning that he could neither elucidate nor suppress. Suzy's face turned pale. She had a bewildered expression on her face. A terrifying thought crossed his mind. What if Suzy could not conceive or worse, tragically lost an offspring and now he had inadvertently opened up old wounds. *Why can I not remember*? He was mentally prepared to offer an apology but the words just would not come out. Instead it was Suzy who spoke first.

'The kids.....yes, the kids.' She paused for a moment. 'They are staying with my parents of course, don't your remember silly? We agreed they would stay at their place for a few days so that they could take in some fresh air by the sea and we could spend some much needed time on our own.... together. My parents will drop them off sometime tomorrow. Isn't it strange that you could forget such a thing.... are you sure you're okay?'

Without waiting for a reply Suzy turned and walked calmly out of the room, closing the door behind her, leaving a bewildered Joslin to his thoughts.

****

Joslin woke at the crack of dawn and immediately turned onto his side so that he could reacquaint himself with Suzy's exquisite features. Although sound asleep the corners of her lips curled upwards to give the illusion that she was smiling contentedly; savouring his display of affection. Recollections of salient moments in their relationship raced through his mind. The day they first met, meeting her parents, Suzy meeting his parents; their wedding day. They were all intense, fond memories, but what should have been the most poignant memories of all - the birth of their children, their first words, first steps and even their physical appearance - had somehow eluded him. He quickly came to the conclusion that he must be a terrible parent. Surely, even when experiencing mild amnesia some memories of the children should be retained? He vowed that he would not dwell on his past parental inadequacies. He would be a much better father from that moment on.

Following a quick shower and full English breakfast Joslin was ready to attend to his chores. Suze was still in bed. Hardly surprising given that he would not allow her a wink of sleep until she had provided comprehensive details of the children's holiday itinerary. He was pleased yet somewhat surprised by the wholly positive feedback. Now, after a surprisingly good night's sleep he was eager to complete his chores early so that he could spend as much time as possible with his family before bedtime.

At mid-day Suzy sauntered over to the barn to inform him that lunch would soon be ready. She decided to stay for a while, humming contentedly to herself while twiddling a single straw between her fingers. He was wondering why it was always so difficult to gauge her mood when an exuberant expression suddenly appeared on her weary face.

'Less than four hours until the children come home. I can't wait! I'd better get their photos and toy's down from the spare bedroom. I'm sorry that I stored them all away. It was rather cold of me but I wanted us to have some time on our own. To make it just like it used to be for a while, with no distractions. You know....just the two of us.'

'Yes, so you said. I suppose I can understand that.'

'I'm sure you're looking forward to the children coming home?' A rhetorical question, nevertheless Joslin was eager to respond.

'Absolutely! I have really missed them.'

'Well,' she said soberly. 'It seems like an eternity since we last set eyes on them. They change so quickly at their age. What do you love most about our wonderful children?'

On posing the question Suzy discarded the straw and made herself comfortable by leaning against the remains of a sycamore tree. Only then did she resume eye contact. She deliberately delayed his riposte until she was ready to interpret the significance of his every word. But what was he to say? Making light of the situation would give credence to the notion that he did not take his parental responsibilities seriously. His only option – though unpredictable – was to say whatever felt appropriate.

'Well, what I love most about our son is that he looks so much like me.' Joslin chuckled nervously before turning to face Suzy; hoping desperately for an indication that he was correct in his assumption. Suzy's barely detectable smile and faint nod of the head put him at ease.

'I also love the way he imitates me in everything I do, and he is curious about everything. Although I sometimes worry that Jake…. Jake's curiosity will get him into trouble one day.'

He chose to ignore Suzy's bemused expression. There was no doubts in his mind that his son was named Jake. It was an instinctive response. His first for some time. Suzy sat up before speaking.

'And what about our other children?' The enthusiasm in his voice was evident as he responded.

'Other *child* not children! We only have one other…..a daughter.' Suzy's face turned red with rage only to appear serene again just seconds later. Only the tone of her voice betrayed her previous demeanour.

'I am perfectly aware of that thank-you very much. What I said could be described as a Freudian slip, given that I did want more…'

'I love that our daughter is extremely beautiful, just like her mother….' Joslin was unaware that he had interrupted Suzy, or that his attempt at flattery was met with disdain. He was caught up in the moment. Euphoric that his narrative had become effortless. It was as though he had somehow tapped into the deep recesses of his mind in order to obtain the answers that were eluding him. He felt compelled to continue.

118

'… and she has a wonderful sense of humour. The way she dances and speaks so eloquently…..' Suzy rose abruptly from her prop. Ostensibly to disrupt his train of thought and convey her displeasure. She was successful on both counts.

'I have to get back to the house now. You clearly do not want to hear what I have to say so I'm not staying here a moment longer listening to you prattle on.'

She strode defiantly towards the farmhouse, but just a few metres into her trek she hesitated before turning to face him once more. The look on her face implied he had already been forgiven.

'I'll ring my parents to find out what time they will be setting off.'

As Suzy walked slowly off into the distance Joslin stood motionless, watching her every movement. He then repeated the same words to himself over and over again, as though he had been placed in a trance. And as he did so his smile grew ever wider. 'Louise….Jake….Louise and Jake… yes, Louise and Jake.'

****

'Where are you going? You can't just go off like this?'

Joslin was expecting a confrontation the moment Suzy spotted him in the driver's seat of the truck. He was mentally prepared for her.

119

'Uhm….and why not? Look, I'm just going into town to get a few things for the children, do you need anything?'

'A few things? Oh you mean presents. No, no…. I'm okay. Well it's good to see you getting out and about again. I hope this means you are getting back to your old self…'

So she had noticed a change in him.

'….but do me a favour and stay away from the town centre or you may miss the children's arrival.'

Joslin's brusque manner seemed to have reassured Suzy but he was not as confident as he appeared. Before starting the engine he instinctively opened the glove compartment and reached for a packet of boiled sweets. Additional probing led to the discovery of a local map. He was delighted to find one. It just might come in handy should his memory fail him again.   As Joslin drove away he caught sight of Suzy waving to him through his wing mirror. When she finally dropped her hand to her side there was a solemn expression on her face. Reminding him of a little girl on her first day at a new school, feeling lost and abandoned.

Engaging the landscape bestowed a sense of serenity that seemed beyond his capacity a few minutes earlier. Ignoring Suzy's advice he bypassed the row of shops that bordered Wolvigston and proceeded towards the lofty steel edifices that comprised a significant portion of the town centre. After parking the truck Joslin strolled through the heart of the shopping complex. Heartened by the friendliness of the shoppers, a number of whom greeted him warmly despite his dishevelled appearance, he found himself wanting to see more of what was on offer.

But the day's work had taken more out of him then he realised. He was visibly tiring and the town square, with its avant-garde layout and infrequent visitors, seemed the ideal place to rest up. While seeking a seating area that would provide adequate shade he noticed a fragile Oak tree, almost hidden behind the branches of much larger and sturdier cedar trees. He might not have noticed it were it not for the fact that its leaves were shimmering brightly under the intense heat of the sun. There was a designated pathway leading to the tree but Joslin was too impatient. Instead he traipsed through the branches of the surrounding tree's knowing it would be an unpleasant experience.

There was something familiar about the oak tree; alluring yet at the same time oddly disturbing. The nearer he came to it the more apprehensive he became. The weather seemed to reflect his changing mood, with the sky clouding over and temperatures falling significantly.

When he came to within a metre of the tree its branches glistened, as though turning to ice. Believing it to be a trick of the light Joslin changed his standing position several times, but to no avail. To the left of the tree there was a stone wall with a plaque attached. It had a black background but the borders and inscription were gilded in gold. A few more steps were needed before he could read the engraving. As he did so a chill went coursing through his spine:

> *'Crossing the Bridge begets eternal happiness or eternal sorrow. Once transcended embrace your destiny, or you and all who accompany you will perish.'*

Unable to interpret it's meaning & increasingly troubled by the hostile environment Joslin found himself struggling to breathe. A barely detectable hum originating from his jacket took him completely by surprise. He retrieved a mobile phone; it must have been placed there by Suzy. The phone call proved a welcome distraction from his feelings of anxiety but he now had to contend with a distraught spouse.

'Where are you? I hope you are not wasting time wandering aimlessly through the town. The children are home and asking for their daddy.'

'I'm sorry Suze. The traffic was terrible and…. I had to turn back for a toilet break.' Joslin winced as he uttered the words. 'I'm on my way home.'

Although grateful that there was little time to mull over what had just happened he was determined to get to the truth, even if meant having to be forthright with Suzy about his memory lapses.

The journey home was a nervy one. His heart rate dictated by his proximity from the farmhouse. The closer he came to it the faster it would beat. He decided to park the truck by the barn where he sat in the dark, with his eyes closed & his head resting gently against the steering wheel. The fact that he had placed such importance on this moment now made it almost impossible to bear. Once again it was the humming of his mobile phone that stunned him into action.

'Hi Suzy, I'm just by the barn…yeah….no…I thought I spotted someone suspicious loitering on our land but I was mistaken. Okay, see you in a minute….bye.'

It was now time for him to act not react. Within seconds the short journey to the farmhouse had been completed and Joslin had one hand firmly on the door handle. As he did so he could hear the sound of children's voices, as they played happily inside.

****

Heads readily turned towards the Kitchen door the moment it sprung open. Two fresh faced children smiled incessantly at Joslin but remained in their seated positions. Louise was sitting at the kitchen table with a doll in one hand and a teddy bear clasped firmly to her chest with the other. On first setting eyes on her father she instantly released her grip on the doll so that it fell lazily onto the wooden table. With her free hand she vigorously scratched at her forehead before hastily snatching up the doll once again.

Jacob was sitting on the floor, perilously close to the open fire with a variety of toys strewn at his feet. Suzy was standing close to Jacob. She too was in smiling mode as she repositioned a family photograph on the mantelpiece. But as she followed Joslin's gaze it dawned on her that he was bitterly disappointed.

'Jacob, Louise! That is no way to greet your father. Why don't you go over and give him a big hug!'

There was a moment's hesitation before they rushed over to provide Joslin with the kind of greeting he had initially hoped for. In their haste Jacob unintentionally bumped into Louise. She fell awkwardly on to the tiled kitchen floor. Suzy intervened.

'Jacob, you must be careful around your little sister. Remember she is a lot younger than you and therefore not as strong as you are.' Joslin leaned forward to hold them both tightly.

'Well, in your rush to give me a cuddle you're falling over each other! It's not very nice for your mother to see but you have now made me a very happy daddy. For a minute there I was beginning to think you had both forgotten who I was.' The irony of his remark was not lost on him.

'I bought you some toys' he said chirpily, 'but unfortunately I left them in the truck.' Suzy shook her head.

'That can wait until tomorrow. They have enough toys from Granny and Granddad to be getting on with.' Suzy's voice trailed off as she spoke. Joslin took this to signify that she would provide little resistance if he were to challenge her judgement.

'No.' he said adamantly. 'I can't wait to see their little faces when they see the wonderful toys I have brought them.'

'Okay, but be careful Joslin. It is pitch black out there.'

Joslin's retreat from the farmhouse was for purely selfish reasons. The reunion failed to produce the infusion of memories he had hoped for, consequently he was finding it increasingly difficult to conceal his disappointment. When he returned to the farmhouse the children wasted no time in greeting him, shouting and giggling with anticipation. Jacob happily held aloft his new toy soldiers; shaking them vigorously in the air.

'Will you play with us Daddy? Please, please!'

'Well, I think I can muster the energy to do that.'

As Joslin, Louise and Jacob played merrily in the kitchen the enticing aroma of a well prepared roast dinner placed their taste buds on full alert. The melodious sound of contemporary classical music in the background and a roaring open fire served to enhance the atmosphere and for the first time since his hangover Joslin was beginning to feel truly *at home*.

One person did not participate in the joviality. Now standing by the kitchen sink Suzy fixated on proceedings much like an exam invigilator monitoring impish students during a lengthy examination. Conversely, as the night wore on and Joslin became engrossed in a string of impromptu activities she too was more at ease, until finally a broad grin could be seen on her increasingly gaunt face.

10

They could not have chosen a more pleasant day for a village fete. Morning conditions could aptly be described as *short sleeves weather* tapered perfectly by a persistent light breeze. But as the day progressed the breeze dissipated and temperatures rose to the extent that even the most excitable adolescents lacked the exuberance expected on such an occasion. The change in environmental conditions contributed to an atmosphere of tranquillity that was more akin to a heart-warming religious convention than an annual gathering of an increasingly transient populace.

The tokens that Suzy had purchased from the administration booth permitted two adults and two children to go on five rides each. Jacob and Louise had just completed their second jaunt on the 'Leviathan' slide and now, with lunchtime approaching the Richards family were on their way to the provisions tent for some much needed sustenance. Before reaching their destination Suzy signalled for Joslin to track her gaze by way of a subtle movement of her head.

'There's Greg. You haven't seen him since your night on the town. Shall we go over and say hello'. Greg was the first person that Joslin instantly recognised since the onset of amnesia, which had to be a good thing. Perhaps this will be the moment when everything finally falls into place.

'I'll go over for a quick chat. Suze…why don't you and the kids get some lunch. Uh… can you get me two sausage rolls and an orange juice? I will be back with you before you know it.'

He could tell by Suzy's body language that she was not best pleased with his course of action. Nevertheless she held tightly to the hands of Jacob and Louise and went on her way.

An animated group of men stood between Joslin and Greg, ostensibly Germanic students judging from their accents and attire. By the time Joslin had manoeuvred his way through to where Greg was standing he decided on a different tact. Rather than greet his friend he would stand his ground and wait for an acknowledgement. It did not take long in coming.

'Joslin. How are you? It's good to see you mate.' Greg almost stumbled in his eagerness to wrap his immense arms around his friend. Joslin appreciated the warm welcome. It seemed like months rather than days since they had seen each other.

'Uh….okay Greg…..you can release me now. You are a lot stronger than you realise.' Joslin could hear the sound of someone panting for breath, standing just behind him.

'Hi Greg how are you? Oh, I got your order Joslin?' Joslin was surprised to see that Suzy and the children had returned so soon.

'It is great to see you Greg' she continued, 'but we had better go back to the tent and find somewhere for the children to sit and eat. No doubt Joslin will be in touch with you soon to arrange another night on the town.' Greg was taken back by her directness.

'Oh, of course...' he eventually replied, 'I understand. Well, see you soon Suzy, Kids...'

In a bid to assist Louise, who was struggling to balance her lunch tray, Joslin made a sudden movement away from his friend. In that moment Greg panicked, ostensibly fearing that there would be no time for a proper good-bye.

'Don't forget to give me a call *JC*!'

'JC?!' The pseudonym suited him perfectly. Even more so after he repeated it a few times. Excited by this revelation he turned to Suzy. Though aware that Joslin's attention was on her it did not prevent Suzy from providing Greg with a menacing stare. She eventually turned to Joslin and smiled.

'Oh, I do so hate it when he calls you that but judging by the look on your face you clearly disagree. Okay Jos…..JC we really have to go.'

Not another word was said to Greg. Nor for that matter between JC and Suzy. At least not until the journey home. By then it had begun to rain. The children read their comic books and calmly played with toys that had taken up permanent residence on the back seats of the truck. Occasionally they would forget themselves in the heat of the moment and voices were raised but one glance from Suzy was enough to ensure that the balance was restored. JC sensed that Suzy was waiting for the right moment before enquiring on his encounter with Greg. But there was nothing to relay. Her prompt return put paid to that. Nevertheless he still considered it to be a breakthrough. What he now needed was time to assess its value. It was Suzy who broke the silence.

'I can't wait to get home and unwind; are you enjoying the music? I can change it if you like.'

'No; I'm good.' He was determined to keep his replies brief.

'It was a good day overall wasn't it?'

'Yes.'

'Well, everything *was* fine until our run-in with Greg.'

'Uh, yeah.' He drove without replying for several minutes.

'What did he do that was so annoying?'

'Oh, just existing.' There was silence.

'I didn't mean it. It's just that I have never really trusted him.'

The children began to argue once more. This time over the ownership of several callously dissected toys. One glance from Suzy would have sufficed but she now had an excuse to vent her anger. All the frustration of the day. The chance meeting with Greg and now strained conversations with JC. It had all taken its toll and now it was the children who were the scapegoats.

'How dare you make such a commotion while we are having a conversation?! We take you on a wonderful day out and you repay us by behaving in such an appalling manner. Well I promise you we will never take you on another......'

The words became irrelevant. It could have been the tone of her voice, or perhaps the feeling of euphoria brought on by seeing Greg again that triggered fresh memories. The emotions that followed were too extreme to be linked to Suzy or even the children who now sat motionless in their seats. He had to compartmentalise these memories first. Be sure he had correctly identified the person responsible for triggering them before speaking out.

'Amanda........yes Amanda. I remember!' It was spoken in a whisper yet Suzy had heard every word. She clasped his arm tightly, which caused the truck to swerve.

'I'm sorry JC. Look...we need to talk. I promise......just as soon as we get home.'

'No, we need to talk now!' He could see it in her eyes. The answers to all those nagging questions were hers to tell and with a little persuading she would be willing to collaborate.

Had JC listened to Suzy's appeal for patience he might have avoided what happened next. Avoided her soul wrenching scream as she suddenly realised they were driving headlong into the path of an oncoming car. But his efforts to manoeuvre back onto the left hand side of the road was being hampered by Suzy, who had inexplicably retained her grip on his arm. He had to find a way of reasoning with her & quickly. JC looked into her eyes for the briefest of moments, providing a reassuring smile. He then calmly spoke her name, certain this would compel her to behave rationally. There was a look of serenity in her eyes as she returned his gaze.

'I love you so much dearie' she whispered dispassionately, 'and I will always be here for you.' Then there was nothing.

****

He was awoken by whispered voices. The more coherent his thoughts became the louder the voices appeared to be.

'The poor man......who's going to give him the news,' He detected a thick northern accent. A second woman, more softly spoken replied in an Australian drawl.

'Mrs Richards was adamant that she would be the one to inform him so we have to respect her wishes.' JC raised himself up onto his elbows.

'Amanda....Amanda.' He barely recognized his own voice. The second woman rushed over to his bedside.

'Mr Richards, please relax. I'm staff nurse Walters, but please call me Becky, and my colleague is Debra. Your wife has just gone to grab a cup of coffee. She will be back shortly.' As they were leaving his private room Debra spoke candidly to her colleague, knowing that she would be overheard.

'He was calling out for Amanda but I'm sure his wife's name is Suzy.'

A few minutes later Suzy entered the room. *Thank God she is alright*! She too was seated in the front of the truck but did not have so much as a scratch on her. Together they had endured most of the impact of the collision & survived so surely the children will also be okay? Suzy stood by his bedside. The look of a lost soul etched on her face. He was heartened by the fact that there were no tears in her eyes.

'Where are the children? I suppose you have left them with your parents until I recover.'

She looked at him in stunned silence.

'What? Please tell me.' Suzy inexplicably interpreted the trace of anxiety in his voice as an indictment on her character. She had no intention of mincing her words.

'I'm afraid they did not make it but I was informed that it would have been relatively painless.'

She did not look him in the eyes. Perhaps she could not cope with an outpouring of grief. Did not wish to be transfixed by his tortured expression, the perfect barometer of his sorrow. It could lead to her feeling vulnerable and exposed too. Just to hear him cry was more than she could bear.

'I…I have to get some tests done, but I'll be back soon. We'll get through this together dearie.' She stooped down to whisper in his ears.

'And remember it was not your fault.'

****

In the days that followed Suzy took control of all outstanding matters. She was concise with her version of events to the authorities. JC believed he had no choice but to concur, and with formal investigations completed it was not long before they returned to a home that was once again a child free environment.

'Where are the children's belongings?' He was dreading seeing their personal effects strewn around the house but it would have been far better than this. The place was immaculate. It even seemed as if the walls in the living room had had been painted a marginally brighter shade of grey. He hastily went from room to room and with each inspection his heart sank even further, until finally he entered the children's shared bedroom.

It had been turned into a study, the walls painted pale red instead of Paris green. A bureau, swivel chair and bookshelf occupied the space where there used to be two beds a toy box and a child-size wardrobe. It was as if they had never existed. JC slowly closed his eyes and shook his head.

'How could you?!' His emotional fragility was of no consequence. Suzy was clinical in her response.

'I thought it would be painful for you to see their belongings in the house as a constant reminder so I had the decorators working their socks off to make sure it was revamped in time for your return home. I was thinking long-term. I didn't think for a minute that you would be *this* upset.'

JC sat on the floor with his back to the wall and his legs fully extended so that his feet were inches away from where Suzy was standing. He sighed before chuckling to himself.

'I need to get away from this place. I also need a drink.'

'I'll come with you.'

'No…no.' He replied brusquely, 'Some time on my own might do me some good. Look…Suzy' She knew what was coming and braced herself.

'.. We need to finish the discussion we began that night in the truck. It did not seem appropriate to discuss it before today but now that the children are *all but forgotten*. Well…we'll discuss it when I return.'

JC rose slowly to his feet and walked pass Suzy without saying a word. She followed him down the stairs and into the kitchen where he poured himself a glass of water at the kitchen sink. Yes, Suzy was upset but he was in no mood to take on board her pain. By the time he reached the replacement truck she was back in the study. This time standing by the window; observing his every move. She anxiously dialled a number on her mobile phone.

'Hello,' she said coolly, 'It's me. Don't talk just listen! I want you to do something for me… for us, and this time don't mess up.'

****

It was one of only two bars in the centre of the village. It was also a Saturday night and yet the venue was barely half full. But JC did not care about those facts, nor did he wish to dwell on the mounting questions streaming through his mind like moths dancing around a bright light. Every face he saw and everyplace he visited seemed to add to the conundrum. More questions and fewer answers. He longed only for solace and the steady consumption of alcohol seemed a reasonable quick fix solution.

There had been times recently when he could look at himself in the mirror without being consumed with guilt. Progress. But those moments were few and far between. If he wished to continue in this vein it would have to be without Suzy. Every time he looked at her his thoughts turned to how calm she had been during those last fateful moments. The way she clung tightly to his arm even though it was hampering his ability to drive. Most distressing of all however was when she blamed him for causing the crash. But why? Perhaps it was her way of gaining control of the situation. Hoping to manipulate him into *towing the line* until she could conjure up a rational explanation for his alternate recollections. If that was indeed the case then her plan had been working perfectly. But no more.

A couple waiting to be served at the bar smiled at him. People always seemed to smile and say a few kind words but no-one seemed willing to engage in conversation. They had been living in the farmhouse for several years yet he knew nobody at the bar. His only friend was Greg, and Suzy did not have any close friends at all. News of their tragic loss must have disseminated around the village by now but they had not received a single message of condolence. Perhaps it was time he left the village altogether!

'Hello JC, I thought I might find you here.'   It was Greg. He had turned up at the bar looking as though he was prepared for a night on the town.

'Hi Greg. Well it looks like we're going to have that drink together sooner than I thought.'

'Yeah sure, but first I've got to tell you that I've spoken to Suzy and she is really worried about you mate. We both are.'

'Why should you be worried?'

'Well I know that you have been having some memory problems. You have been through a lot in recent times... and our friendship. I know we've had our ups and downs but what matters is that we've come through the other end stronger than ever. We'll down a few pints and swap lies as always but at the end of the night I'm making sure that you get home safely and in one piece.'

'Well I would drink to that but my glass is empty and seeing as I can't remember who bought the last round between us, I'll just assume it's your turn. The bar is that way.'

Just a few seconds with Greg proved more informative than the last few weeks with Suzy. So Greg knew of the gaps in his memory. Did Suzy inform him after the road accident or had he been aware for some time? Perhaps even before their last drinking session? This was a unique opportunity for him to gather intelligence before confronting Suzy. It all seemed so simple in theory. Greg was evidently in a reflective mood so all he had to do was keep him drinking and talking. But JC was unwilling to revise his own drinking pattern. He had already been drinking heavily and it was not long before his vision became hazy and his movements erratic. The last thing he remembered was being lead out of the bar by Suzy. He asked her why she had turned up but she merely smiled politely and suggested they take a taxi home. JC's night was over but his lamenting would inevitably continue.

****

The following morning JC woke with a thumping headache. He immediately turned onto his side to see if Suzy was beside him. His senses toiled in the dark until he detected her presence. She was sitting at the end of the bed, facing the window, swaying gently back and forth like a travel sick car passenger desperately trying to take their mind off the journey.

'Good morning, JC....we need to talk. I'll wait for you in the kitchen.' Without uttering another word she rose slowly from the bed and exited the room.

He sensed that this was the moment. The moment when the answers to all those nagging questions would be revealed. But why now? It seemed absurd to be negative at a time like this, but having existed in a state of uncertainty for so long did he really need to know the truth right now? If it was more bad news could he really cope with it so soon after their recent loss? He walked slowly down the stairs, his thoughts erratic, considering ways to delay or permanently put a stop to the revelations. When he arrived at the kitchen door Suzy was standing by the sink. She was staring out of the window. He thought it best to speak first.

'Suzy I.....'

'No, let me explain everything Joslin then you can say your piece. You...you have been suffering from delusions for a number of years now. I had hoped that we were winning the battle; beginning to get it under control but now I see that we have failed yet again.'

'What?!'

'I know this will come as a shock to you, but it is your third...no fourth relapse and now I just don't know what to do anymore.' JC was not sure what he had expected her to say, but it certainly was not this.

'I know I've had problems remembering things lately and I should have spoken to you about it sooner, but I am not delusional! Perhaps you should rewind a little and tell me exactly what you think is going on!' She turned to face him for the first time that morning.

'Yes of course. Well, we were a happy couple to begin with, and a happy family for a number of years. Then out of the blue you began constructing an imaginary world in which you were the central character. You had an alternate family and friends. A beautiful model partner, or was she a minor celebrity, by the name of Amanda and two perfect children. We became mere acquaintances to you. For the last two years we have been working with a psychiatrist, a Dr Carmichael in an attempt to reverse the effects.

The children staying with my parents and putting their things away in the toy room was all part of the rehabilitation process.

We thought you were beginning to make progress, and I hoped that we could be a proper family again. It was working…for a while, but lately you have been saying things which led me to believe that the delusions were manifesting once again. And then the accident. You were driving on the wrong side of the road for goodness sake?!'

He had perceived the incident a little differently but could see no value in arguing the point.

'It's true that I have been having strange thoughts and feelings lately'. He said hesitantly,

'I didn't quite know how they fitted in with us as a family. They seemed so….real.' Suzy's expression changed. There was hope in her eyes.

'Perhaps I'll give Dr Carmichael a call and we could give it one more try. You will give it a real go this time and do exactly what the Doctor says…won't you?'

JC nodded in agreement. What Suzy had told him was disconcerting but it made sense. By her definition he had been slipping further away from reality with each passing day. He was able

140

to visualise his 'other' family so clearly now, and recollect the little things that made them seem so real. The scent of their hair and their mannerisms. He could even remember reading the children their favourite bedtime stories. The children....

'I will make every effort to get better Suzy. Maybe this is the best time to do it with all these painful memories of the twins still fresh in my mind. Hopefully he can make it all go away.'

A broad smile spanned Suzy's face. She turned towards the kitchen sink and briefly rubbed her hands, as though she was about to tackle the washing up. But there were no plates or kitchen utensils in the sink and besides, he had not quite finished talking.

'I just called the children twins and you did not even bat an eyelid.'

'...That's because they are...were twins silly.'

'That's not what you said on the night they came back home from your parents. I distinctly remember you describing Louise as Jacob's little sister, claiming she was a lot younger than him, and you were right. She is... was clearly younger than him by at least two years. But in my so-called delusional state the children are the same age. They look the same age. The same height. So which is it Suzy?

There was silence for what seemed an eternity. Then quite unexpectedly Suzy began to laugh.

'Well, I suppose I have myself to blame. They advised me to read your dossier but what was the point. You were not supposed to remember a damn thing! Besides I did not want to waste my time thinking about your so-called family. They were irrelevant. They still *are* irrelevant. All I care about is you....'

11

It was as though the pivotal scene from a crime novel was reached. The one where the shrewd, persistent detective smugly informs everyone connected to the case how and why the crime had been committed. The only onlooker on this occasion was JC, but his ability to perform the role of a bewildered, self-effacing pawn was faultless. He sat motionless on the sofa, head bowed, trying to rationalise what was being said, but as Suzy elaborated on the extent of the conspiracy JC came to realise that he was not totally blameless.

'.....though our relationship could be described as a complete sham that was not always the case. Oh, I can tell by the look on your face that you still do not remember me. Well perhaps this will jog your memory. Our relationship began eleven years ago when you were nineteen years old and I was thirty-two.'

'Thirty-two? I think I would remember that.' He wanted to laugh out loud. To tell Suzy how absurd she was being, but the tone of her voice abetted by the sincere look on her face compelled him to be silent.

'When we first met you immediately assumed I was just a few years older than you. I was flattered and saw no reason to tell you the truth. While we were together I became pregnant and I...we had a daughter, Abigail. I was going to tell you about the pregnancy but first I needed to be sure you wanted me for who I was, and not because you felt obligated. That was my first mistake, allowing sentiment to cloud my judgement. A few days after discovering I was pregnant I overheard some of your friends discussing your exploits at a local nightclub. How you frequently left with a different girl on your arm. They also spoke of an older woman you were stringing along.'

Suzy casually walked over to where JC was seated, hoping to gauge his response. She huffed and shook her head when he spurned the opportunity to make eye contact.

'I should be grateful that I was spared the big break-up scene. The one when I say 'how could you' and you consistently lie through your teeth before ending with the pathetic 'it's not you it's me' speech. I was only spared that embarrassment because you stopped coming around to see me. Not a word. No visits. No phone call. Nothing.'

JC thought he should make an effort to defend himself even though his heart was not in it.

'Let's just say you are telling the truth about our shared history. Well, yes I was pretty horrible back then but I was just a kid having fun and not considering the consequences. Just like any other guy my age.'

'Ah yes, but then you became a man and you continued with your antics.' Stunned by the veracity of her riposte he unwittingly resumed eye contact.

'Oh yes, I have been monitoring your exploits with great interest, and it seems to me that you continued to trample on the feelings of others until….until…'

'Until Amanda,' he said conceitedly. 'See I have changed.' It was Suzy's turn to be taken back.

'I see your memory is improving, only now you seem to be suffering from selective memory. Granted your relationship with Amanda was progressing relatively well. But then …oh, what was her name…that's right *Maisie* came along. Can you see now? It does not matter who you are with you will never change. At least while you are here with me I can save you from yourself.'

Bewilderment turned once again to anger. He was angry that she knew so much about him and was passing judgment yet he knew very little about her. This was taking far too long.

'Where am I and where is my real family?' A mischievous look appeared on Suzy's face.

'Okay dearie, one question at a time. In answer to your first question I would have to say that it is all in your mind.' JC swiftly rose to his feet. He had run out of patience.

'No more games pl…'

'Calm down JC.' She calmly intervened. 'I am being sincere when I say that it is quite literally *all* in your mind. Do you remember the party that you attended at Wrex Tower? It was held on a Friday night at the end of your first week back at work?'

'Yes,..yes!'

'You were taken to the basement by ….'

'Kate! Kate Pritchard. We used the special elevator and...... I was drugged!'

'Honestly JC don't be so dramatic. Kate was merely following orders. My orders. After all I am *the* majority shareholder of the Company. Kate was merely easing you through the early stages of the crossover process. A process that led you here, to the people who truly love you.'

Suzy took a deep breath before continuing.

'You are here with us ....well, in spirit. Your physical form is currently in a state of induced coma. Our bodies, mine and one other person, are lying beside yours in the Anti-chamber in the Wrex Tower basement. It is believed that the closer we are to you - the host - during the initial phase of the crossover the more successful the bonding will be.' The look of horror on his face unnerved Suzy.

'Please don't look at me like that! It had to be this way so that our minds would be linked. We wanted to be with you for all time and this was the only way we knew how. But don't worry the ritual itself has stood the test of time. In fact it dates back centuries. Royalty, rich noblemen and famous people associated with our fraternity have followed the same path. Their bodies eventually decay but their minds still live on, residing in their notion of utopia.'

'Being a farmer in a backwater town is not really my idea of utopia!' Suzy perceived his flippant response as a positive development.

'I know it wasn't your idea. I wanted everything to be on my terms and I'm sorry. I have always wanted to live on a farm but never got around to it, until now. But you have the ability to manipulate this world. Turn it into anything you want it to be. We can move to another town, a big city or even a beautiful sunny island if you like. It will take a little time but the world is your oyster.' He sighed.

'That's just the problem. This is not my world. You say my body is still functioning so how do I return to it?'

'Return?' she replied dismissively. 'There is no return. You will just have to learn to adapt to this new existence. We love you and in time our daughter may also join us. I want her to live a little first, maybe she will find happiness in the real world. If not then she knows what must be done when the time is right.'

His heart sank to immeasurable depths when she uttered those chilling words. To think that he will never again witness Amanda's beautiful smile nor hold his beloved children in his arms was too much to bear. Then there was Maisie. She was so good to him, and for him. He would never be able to apologise for dismissing her feelings so callously. Suzy was alert to the look of resignation in his eyes, and wondered what was going through his mind. She needn't have worried. There was just one word to describe what he was feeling at that moment; acceptance. JC's days of being in control of his destiny was over. There was just one more question he needed to ask.

'Who are you?'

'Who am I?'

'Yes, who are you?'

Tears trickled down Suzy's cheeks as she struggled to come to terms with the fact that he still could not recall their time together. It was a temporary blip. As was often the case with Suzy her mood quickly changed and the acidic temper, an all too frequent feature of their unique relationship re-emerged with a vengeance:

'I'll tell you who I am dearie. I'm the woman who gave you private tuition when you fell behind at College. I'm the woman who ensured you received good grades in not only Math's, your weakest subject, but also Physics and Chemistry even though I was not being paid to do so. I'm also the woman who wanted to make you a partner in my newly created firm. We could have been partners in business as well as our personal life but you did not even bother to take my offer seriously.'

She paused for a moment. When she spoke again it was slower and more deliberate, with a softer tone. It was as if she had practiced verbalising what she was about to say a thousand times.

'JC…I..I did everything I could to make things develop naturally between us. At one stage I thought we were becoming really close at the café. I could tell that you had feelings for me but for some reason you were holding back.

'The café? You are Gloria from the café?! But she's….old!' She responded surprisingly well to his unflattering remark.

'During the ritual it is possible to look like anyone we choose to in the eyes of the host person. I chose to be myself when I was twenty five years old. You found me attractive at thirty-two so why not even more so at twenty five?' JC did not respond. He was still finding it difficult to come to terms with the situation. Instead he chose to reflect on how a more fitting punishment could not have been devised. He will spend eternity with someone who was delightful to behold but her true nature - obsessive, manipulative and controlling - will be a constant reminder of his failure to provide the numerous women he had known with the respect they deserved.

'Yes,' He responded meekly. 'I do remember you now and our time together.'

Relieved that the pretence was over and heartened by JC's acquiescence Suzy spoke candidly.

'Can you imagine that no-one back in the real world knows for certain that the process works. Although there are numerous accounts of individuals that have miraculously regained consciousness and spoken of a world resembling our own but infinitely better. Some actually believed they had been to heaven. Just imagine! I took the gamble. I dared to cross over the bridge and it paid off. I guess that's what spiritual guru's would call having blind faith.'

'What did you say?' JC rose suddenly from his seated position, his eyes appearing to increase significantly in both size and intensity. The sense of urgency that emanated through every fibre of his being convinced Gloria that she had made a dreadful error. What could it have been? A word? An expression? Or even a gesture may have been enough to give him renewed hope. She followed JC as he walked confidently out of the house via the back door and towards the truck, deviating only to collect his recently sharpened axe. Now panic stricken, Gloria was determined to regain control of the situation. She placed herself between JC and the truck door.

'Please tell me what's going through your mind. Maybe I can help?' JC hesitated. There was a distant look in his eyes, as though he was being instinctively guided to somewhere that was previously out of his grasp; perhaps towards his old life. Wherever it was it would not include Gloria.

'You are not going anywhere until you tell me what is going on!' A wry smile crossed his face.

'I know.'

'Know…know what?'

'You spoke of having crossed over the bridge. I've seen a sign alluding to that very fact by the old Oak Tree in the town square. I knew I had seen that tree somewhere before but could not remember where…until now.' A look of horror crossed Gloria's face.

'You didn't tell me that you had gone into town!' He was in no mood to digress.

'That night in the basement, just before I passed out, I remember seeing an Oak Tree. It was shimmering just like the one in Town. The weaker I became the brighter it appeared to glow.' Gloria's expression implied that she intended to deride his supposition, but it was quickly replaced with a look of resignation.

'Okay you got me, but you need to understand the history of the tree before you do anything silly.'

'I'm listening.' There was a momentary pause before she cleared her throat then calmly made her case:

'The Oak tree is central to our existence on this plane. It is an ancient, mystical tree that is linked to two vastly different but equally extraordinary origins. Some say it was seized by the Romans from Druids based in Anglesey during their subjugation of Britain in the first century AD. Though secretly revered by the Roman elite they had no idea of its true potential.

There are also claims that the tree originated in Norway and was the inspiration behind the legend of Yggdrasil, also known as the 'World Tree' in Norse mythology. Scandinavian adherents to our cause went to great lengths to conceal its identity with later portrayals' depicting it as an Ash rather than Oak tree. It was transported to England in the 12th Century, and has been utilised by our Sacred Order ever since.

I don't know if either of these origins have any validity but I am certain of one thing. The Tree forms a gateway between the world we now exist in and the real world. The tree in this world is a psychic manifestation of the real one but equally as important. If it is harmed in any way then there is a strong possibility that *we will die in both worlds!*'

'A possibility?' he anxiously replied. 'Well if there is even a remote chance that I can return home then it is a risk worth taking.' Gloria seemed perplexed. She had hoped her explanation would at the very least make JC consider his options. Thus providing her with time to resolve their differences.

'I need to make a phone call JC.'

'What?!'

'I know it sounds crazy but just give me a few minutes to make a call. It's important. You never know, after you have heard all the facts you might just change your mind.'

Gloria hurried back to the house. She glanced back twice. On both occasions it was to plead with JC to wait. *Wait for what? - More lies*! The time for waiting was over. He would now take matters into his own hands. JC got into the truck and drove. In his wing mirror he could see Gloria running out of the house with mobile phone in hand. She then returned to the house. No doubt to collect the keys to the hatchback. It was much quicker than the truck so he needed to take full advantage of his slender head start.

*****

It was not quite mid-day yet the sky resembled dusk; the darkest stage of twilight. Temperatures had dropped considerably. The roads and shopping precincts were devoid of people. It was as if there was a general acceptance that the end was inevitable, but for who? Will it merely herald the end of his existence in this reality or will he actually be committing suicide? JC drove straight to the town square, committing numerous traffic violations on the way. He parked the truck on the pavement, deliberately blocking the entrance to the square. When he arrived at the ancient Oak Tree it was shimmering intensely. The effect bordering on hypnotic; it was as though he was being beckoned and repelled in equal measures. JC held the axe high above his head but he was not prepared to strike a blow. He needed time to compose himself. He could hear the arrival of a car and then a few seconds later another, heavier vehicle; most likely a truck. Before long he was joined by Gloria and a second individual.

'Greg! Gloria brought you here. But why?'

'Because she believes that only I could talk some sense into you. Look, JC if you harm that tree in any way you could kill us all. Now what would be the point of that?'

JC laughed hysterically. The sound of his voice reverberating frostily in the increasingly soulless environment.

'I've got news for you Greg, you do not really exist. You are quite literally a figment of my imagination....well either that or Gloria's cronies conjured you up to make this existence more tolerable for me.'

'No-one created me *Don Juan*. I am here because I choose to be.' Only one person had ever called him Don Juan. The moment the words were uttered JC's jaw dropped. The axe fell gently from his hand.

'Lenny; is it really you! How?'

'Well perhaps you should be asking why. If you read my farewell note you will know how difficult I was finding it to carry on. Gloria first contacted me during my disciplinary hearing at North Sac International. You know....after I assaulted Reeves. She persuaded the board to give me another chance and ensured that Reeves' was handsomely compensated for his troubles, and for his silence. Even the police were civil to me during my interrogation. Gloria's influence extends all the way to the top in both organisations.' Lenny and Gloria turned to face one another and smiled.

'You see Gloria realised how important our friendship was and that I helped to keep you grounded while you made me feel positive about myself. But Gloria and I never spoke again until shortly after our falling out in the canteen. She contacted me. Told me of her crossover plans and the role I would play; being your best friend once again. At first I thought she was crazy, but then I was given a tour of her business empire. I even worked for her for a while. You see... once the ritual was explained in detail I realised that she really was in love with you. We are two people who are willing to sacrifice all for someone we deeply care for.'

JC's hands began to tremble. To prevent this aberration he slowly clenched his fists.

'But….we all believed you had died. Amy thought you were dead! She cares a lot more for you than you realise.'

'Amy? I...I cared a lot for her too. But I suppose I did die in a way. I took an overdose, and if the doctors had miscalculated I would not be here today. I was placed in an induced coma.'

'Let me guess. The Doctors in attendance were on Gloria's payroll?' Without waiting for a response JC turned to face Gloria.

'So you made a slightly younger version of Lenny too. He looks just like he did in the photos I saw in his apartment. That's probably why I immediately recognized him. Felt a connection. Tell me Gloria, how did you know that I would apply for the Office manager's position? And how did you manage to get Kate to lure me into the basement?'

'You mustn't blame Kate, she had no choice. I am the majority shareholder of the Company. She is employed to do exactly as she is told. As for you applying for the job, well I was aware of your financial difficulties and the type of roles you were applying for so I ensured that a position became available at the Company that offered an exorbitant salary. My personal assistant informed Daphne at the Employment Agency that we wanted you for the post but to make it seem that you were doing the manipulating. I know how you like to be in control.' JC shook his head.

'You have gone to an awful lot of trouble to create this reality Gloria. I suppose I should be flattered. The one good thing about this situation is that I have been given a chance to see you again Lenny, if only to apologize for the way that I treated you. You were my best friend who would never do anything to harm me and I took advantage of that. I will never forgive myself for what I did to you for as long as I…exist.' Lenny smiled and nodded.

'Gloria…' JC reached down for the axe as he addressed her.

'…you should have told me about our daughter. It may have helped me to grow up sooner and take responsibility for my actions. You may not have noticed but I have changed in recent years. Became a responsible adult, raising two beautiful children. I think I have done a pretty good job with them so far, now I would like to continue the job…. or die trying.'

He struck hard at the tree. Once the first blow had been struck there was no turning back. His swinging motion turned into a wild frenzy. The shimmering intensified as branches now laid strewn at his feet. JC could not be sure if it was his mind playing tricks or reality setting in but he thought he heard the voices of children. His children, shouting his name, calling on him to return. The last thing he was certain that he heard, apart from Gloria's frantic screams, was the remarkably composed voice of Lenny.

'Thank you for apologizing JC, it means the world to me. I understand why you are doing this and I…I hope you make it back.'

On hearing those words tears formed in JC's eyes. He had neither the strength nor energy to continue his assault, but the damage had been done. The shimmering stopped and only darkness prevailed. Then there was nothing.

Part Three

Facing Reality

12

He can remember making the phone call, hearing the sound of her voice and knowing that she desperately needed to talk to him. But he hung up. Then there was the letter he wrote to her explaining precisely why their relationship would never work. He never posted it. His failure to converse with Gloria and help her find closure triggered a series of events that had dire consequences. The psychological effect on him was severe. So severe that he was genuinely relieved to be distracted from his thoughts by the intensity of the sun's rays as it breached the hitherto impenetrable dense red curtains.

Still too weary to open his eyes JC's other senses were occupied by unexpected distractions. The ubiquitous odour of sanitary products and the jarring sound of clanking metal, but it was the voices that disturbed him most of all. Their frenzied dispersal reminded him of his childhood. Of a Sunday afternoon in a tiny Council flat when outdoor activities were curtailed by the winter weather. He would remain silent. Motionless, for what seemed like an eternity while his father anxiously tinkered with the dials of his analogue radio in a vain attempt to simultaneously keep abreast of live football and cricket scores.

It was quite a struggle but he eventually opened his eyes. He was not in his bedroom on the farm. Instead of red curtains there were white blinds, adjusted to let in the light. The clanking sounds originated from metal hospital beds that were being re-made to accommodate new patients. He was now able to focus his attention on the faces that were closest to him. Those making the loudest sounds. It was the voices of children. *His* children and Amanda. He had returned home. It was Amanda who spoke the first words that he was able to interpret.

'Hi handsome, you made it back. I knew you would…..Children get off the bed! Jacob do not hug daddy too tightly, you could do him some damage.'

'A-Amanda, it's really you.' She laughed enthusiastically. Her amusement at his capacity to state the obvious augmented by a profound sense of relief.

'The children never gave up on you. They spoke to you endlessly, almost every day.'

'And you?' It was not what he said but the way he way he said it that was regrettable. Now was not the time for recrimination. Fortunately Amanda did not hear him over the din of the children. Either that or she simply chose to ignore the remark.

'The Doctor should be back in a few minutes,' she said softly. 'We've been told not to tire you out, so we'll wait for an update and then I'll take these two terrors home. Don't worry, I'll return later on my own and we can have a proper chat.'

It was exactly what he wanted to hear. Too exhausted to engage in protracted dialogue JC still needed to be sure he was back in the *real world* as soon as possible. To do that he must ready himself for their first meaningful conversation. Catch her off guard if need be.

Doctors came and went bringing nothing but good news. Early indications revealed no permanent physical or psychological damage. Encouraged by the news JC made a valiant attempt to consume some broth soup. He then slept. After what seemed like a matter of minutes he was awoken by a chirpy Amanda. She leaned over to kiss him on the forehead.

'Hi handsome, I'm back.'

'Hi buttercup.'

'Buttercup? Mmmm…. do I look like a flower to you? Maybe I should have another word with the Doctor, just to make sure that you are JC and not a bumblebee hoping to get lucky and pollenate.'

It was a typical retort from Amanda, and one that immediately put him at ease.

'What happened to me Amanda? What do you know?'

'Not a lot really, but it must have been one heck of a party at Wrex Tower! Apparently you were brought in by a couple wearing strange gowns. They did not say who they were, just dropped you off and left.'

'When was this?'

'The night of the party…well the morning after to be precise.'

It was not a lot to go on but it did make a good deal of sense. Gloria inferred that the *Crossover* was more likely to succeed if the participants remained in close proximity to one another. JC's abduction at a crucial stage in the ritual would explain how he was able to retain memories of people and places in the real world.

Amanda leaned forward in her chair. She was clearly enthused by what she was about to convey.

'I have just heard the strangest news. The major shareholder from your place of work, Gloria Danewood passed away today. It happened in Wrex Tower at midday. Virtually the same time that you were coming out of your coma.'

How was he meant to respond to such an announcement? Unaware of his distress Amanda continued.

'It gets even more bizarre. An unidentified man who was also in the building at the time has been brought into this hospital. This hospital! He is currently on a life support machine. The police say that the two incidents are unrelated. It's all over the news.'

The speed at which the information was being transmitted added to his sense of bewilderment. All the things he had seen and done since entering the elevator that night, could they really have happened? He turned to Amanda and delivered an ungainly expression before speaking.

'Can you be a dear and bring in some clothes for me?'

'What?! You're not going anywhere until the doctors say so.'

It was essential that he maintained his composure; continue to converse in a courteous yet no-nonsense manner. That was how he usually performed on the rare occasions that he got his own way with Amanda.

'The doctors have told me that I need to take some light exercise and the sooner the better. I am being encouraged to walk around the grounds, but you know what I'm like. I am not going to do that in my pyjamas. If you could pop home now then I could go for a stroll in the morning......around the gardens.'

It seemed a reasonable request. She smiled, nodded and got up to leave.

'Oh and just one more thing Amanda. Can you bring me that photo that you like so much? The one of me with my drinking buddies from North Sacs International..........It's on the bookshelf.

****

It was all going to plan. After visiting hours were over JC rested for a while to conserve energy. When he woke at nine o'clock pm the ward was quiet. The on duty medical staff noticeable by their absence. He went to the bathroom and changed into the clothes that Amanda had brought in; a jumper, jeans, trainers and a denim jacket. He then returned to his bedside to collect his wallet, watch and some spare change. Within a few minutes he will be taking a cab ride to Wrex Tower. No doubt he will be castigated on his return, but it would all be worth it if evidence was uncovered that gave credence to his version of events. Preparations

163

had been going so well that he became complacent, and failed to notice a slender figure standing motionless, just inches from his bedside cabinet.

'Where do you think you are going, JC?' The words were whispered yet he immediately recognised the voice.

'Maisie! How? Why are you here?!' She smiled nervously and the warmth and energy that only she could emit seemed to illuminate the poorly lit ward. He turned to look her squarely in the eyes but a sharp twinge in his back made him flinch.

'Come on, I'll help you onto the bed. What on earth do you think you were doing?' He flinched once more as Maisie placed a second pillow under his head.

'There is something that I need to do Maisie. It's very important.'

'But not as important as your health.' They looked at each other for what seemed an eternity. No words were said but it was obvious that they were pleased to see each other.

'Look, I'm sorry that I startled you JC but I needed to make sure you were okay. I...I've been coming to see you every night since I discovered you were in a coma.' JC suddenly realised he had no idea how long it had been since the party.

'Three weeks and two days! You've been coming to see me every night for three weeks and two days?'

'No. I had no idea you were in a coma for the first two days. It was only after Tony told me.

You remember Tony? A Jamaican chap; he usually visits the Eden park play area with his two daughters. The girls always have their hair plaited in one long ponytail.' JC had no idea who she was talking about.

'Yes, I remember him... vaguely.'

'Tony's a nurse at the hospital. He overheard some colleagues talking about a really cute patient that was in a coma, so he went to see what all the fuss was about and immediately recognized you. He arranges for me to see you when no-one is around.' There was a moment's silence.

'I hope you don't feel that I am stalking you. I just wanted....needed to see for myself that you were alright.'

JC could feel his heart beating erratically, but not because of what Maisie had said but for what he was about to say.

'I am really glad to see you again, particularly after the way we parted. On that day I....I did not express my feelings in the way that I should have, or the way that I wanted to, and uh, well....it could have gone a lot better.'

Maisie chuckled loudly. Then, remembering where she was hurriedly placed her hands over her mouth in an exaggerated manner. They waited until the other patients on the ward had stopped stirring in their beds before continuing.

'Well it's not like you to rattle on,' she whispered. 'I'm not sure what you meant by all that but I'm going to assume you are expressing how happy you are now that we are talking again. Well I am too.'

Maisie's smile was reciprocated. On the surface it was no different to the way they had gazed at each other on numerous occasions. But there was an innocence bordering on naivety that pervaded their interaction. Compelling JC to behave in a manner that he was unaccustomed too. Without warning a pensive expression overwhelmed Maisie's delicate features.

'I saw Amanda as she was leaving today. Wow! Didn't realise TV presenter & weather girl Amanda was your partner. You kept that quiet! She is even more beautiful in the flesh. I could never compare to someone like her.' JC shook his head.

'Don't sell yourself short, Maisie. Granted you are a little bit weird...' They both giggled, '...but you are beautiful in ways that I never really believed were possible.

The look of surprise on her face did not deter JC from what he wanted to say. 'It's true Maisie, you are always genuine, caring and you never play emotional games. What you see is what you get as they say, and it's very refreshing.'

'Thank you,' she replied, 'but your remark about not playing games is not entirely true. We are all game players to some degree, but I'm just not very good at it because I will always wear my heart on my sleeves.' Maisie rose from her chair as though intending to leave, then hesitated. She leaned forward, speaking nervously. Almost inaudibly.

'Promise me you will not leave the hospital tonight?'

Touched by her level of concern JC sat up in bed and slowly manoeuvred his torso so that his feet dangled inches from the floor.

'I promise, but in return you must do something for me.' Maisie nodded.

'I need Tony to check up on a patient for me.'

'Sure, what's the name?' JC shook his head.

'He would not have been brought in under his real name.'

He leaned forward, towards the bedside cupboard and picked up the photograph that Amanda had brought in earlier that day.

'A man was admitted today from Wrex Tower and is currently in a coma. I want to know if it is this person on the left in this photograph.' A confused look emerged on Maisie's face.

'Another coma patient. JC, what's going on?'

'Probably nothing if the face does not match. If it does then I promise that I will tell you everything this time tomorrow. That is if you can make it?

13

There was so much to look forward to on that bright Autumnal day. An extended visit by Amanda and the children. The prospect of further improvements in his mobility and now that his appetite had returned he could resume eating solids. Yet there was more than a hint of apprehension in his deliberation. A ghastly notion that would not go away. *What if he was still trapped in the world that Gloria had created*? If that was the case then his poignant conversation with Lenny prior to the destruction of the ancient oak tree was contrived. Most likely to lure him into a false sense of security. It horrified him to think that Gloria could still be out there, somewhere behind the scenes. Pulling the strings of everyone he came into contact with.

He needed to remain alert. Look for signs of anomalies, but most importantly of all he must take the initiative. Take whatever steps was needed to get to the truth in the shortest period of time.

The time spent with Amanda, Jake and Louise was filled with laughter. There was a lot of catching up to do and the adults were happy to let the children take the lead. JC's optimism endured right up until Amanda's unaccompanied return later that evening. It was his own fault. He knew the timing was wrong yet he did not wish to persist with meaningless small talk when, from his perspective at least, their relationship was on the line. So he questioned Amanda about the text she received *that* night. The night that changed his life forever.

'So you've been reading my texts.' She replied angrily. 'I'm the one who should be annoyed with you and not the other way around!'

JC did not rise to the bait. One misplaced remark could exacerbate the situation and he may never again have the opportunity to get to the truth. He waited for the silence to become deafening; only then would the feeling of guilt overwhelm her.

'It's not what it seems,' she finally exclaimed.

'Ray is a colleague and... well... A few of us from work got together regularly for drinks. I did not lie about meeting my old University friends. They came along too. Not all the time but occasionally.'

JC took a deep breath before asking the question they both knew was coming.

'Did you sleep with him?'

'No.' The response was instantaneous but it was conveyed in a way that implied there was a little more to it. JC was surprised how easy it was to interpret Amanda's mood, her body language and even what she was about to say. Perhaps, he thought sombrely, it was because he had been in her situation on numerous occasions in the past. But now the boot was on the other foot. Amanda bided her time before continuing. Choosing her words carefully.

'It was not that kind of relationship, if you can even call it a relationship at all. It was more a meeting of minds.' JC promptly sat up in bed.

'Meeting of minds...,' he said nonchalantly.

'..Some might say that is even more worrying.'

He could tell by the look on Amanda's face that he had struck a chord, yet he was finding it impossible to be angry with her. How could he when his deductions was predicated on *his* own recent experience with another women? Confronting his feelings was still an alien concept to him, yet he was coming to realise that emotions cannot always be pushed to one side simply because you have pre-existing obligations. Making mistakes is human but it is how you respond thereafter that defines a relationship.

He recalled how a chance encounter several years ago had opened his heart to the notion of taking a chance and engaging in a long-term relationship. Had he not met Amanda he might never have experienced the unconditional love that he now had for his children. Conversely he might not have been so susceptible to Suzy's bizarre notion of domestic bliss or have established a blossoming, yet indefinable relationship with Maisie. Good, bad or indefinite these were experiences that he had previously been incapable of having. Now he was exposed and taking risks with his emotions just like everyone else, and he was grateful. Knowing all this how could he possibly sit in judgement of her?

'You talk about your relationship with this …Ray in the past tense. Perhaps we should leave all thoughts on what happened between the two of you in the past as well. I know the pressures you have been under over the last few years and lately, having to look after Jacob and Louise on your own. But we've both made mistakes. Here's hoping that we have learned from them and can move on.'

Relieved by his response Amanda attributed JC's magnanimity to his near death experience. She was only partially correct in her assumption. Nevertheless, a pivotal moment in their relationship had been reached. A new found respect for one another emerged that day, but it was one that was based as much on their shared history and love for one another as it was on their increasing differences.

****

Ever since parting company with Maisie the night before he marvelled at the difference a day made. For weeks JC had taken alternate routes to and from home to avoid her in the belief that an encounter - no matter how brief - would be an uncomfortable experience for both parties. But their meeting was nothing of the kind. She did not exactly promise to meet with him that evening, but he hoped. Once visiting time was over he slept, and dreamed of obtaining answers to the more pertinent question that had annexed all corners of his mind.

'Hi JC, how are you?' His eyes opened wide as soon as he heard Maisie's voice.

'Sorry to wake you but you did say that you wanted to see me tonight.' JC quickly raised himself onto his elbows.

'Of course …Uh Hi. I wasn't really asleep. It's great to see you.'

Maisie did not reply or even return his smile. Instead she handed him the photograph he had given her the night before.

'Yes, he is the John Doe. Apparently he has lost a few pounds since it was taken but it is definitely him.' A wry smile crossed JC's face.

'So Lenny is alive. It really did happen.'

'Lenny! Your best friend Lenny?! There's something else.…'

'Sorry to interrupt,' he said abruptly, 'but I believe I owe you an explanation and I'd like to give it to you now while I still have the courage to do so. I just hope you don't think that I am totally mad at the end of it.'

After a lengthy explanation was made Maisie sat motionless for what seemed an eternity, without saying a word.

'You don't believe me do you?' JC's words evoked a look of irritation from Maisie, but it was pursued by a broad smile and her all-to-familiar cheeky grin.

'I think you're forgetting that deep down I am a child of the sixties, and in those day's *weird* stuff happened all the time. Although normally a hallucinogenic drug was the trigger. Besides, what you say, as weird as it may sound would explain a lot.' Although she had perked up JC could see that she was struggling with something.

172

'Come on Maisie out with it. You can tell me.'

She took a sharp intake of breath before responding.

'I was about to tell you a moment ago but you interrupted me. Your friend….Lenny, has disappeared.'

'Disappeared! What do you mean disappeared?'

'Apparently he was showing signs of re-gaining consciousness. Everything was fine when the nurse checked on him at mid-day but, less than an hour later he was reported missing. The police have been checking through CCTV footage hoping for a lead.'

JC pushed the bed sheets to one side and sat grim faced on the edge of the bed. He spoke with such passion that it became impossible to continue whispering.

'I think it's obvious who has taken him! Don't you see? Lenny and I are probably the only people alive to have crossed over and survived. If one of us was to inform the authorities of our experience we could be portrayed as a fantasist; unstable. But together we just might be taken seriously….. Lenny has been through so much. He doesn't deserve this.'

JC thought long and hard on what he was about to ask Maisie. It could endanger her life, but if his theory was correct then Maisie's clandestine visits to his bedside would not have gone unnoticed. She may already be a target. Maisie took the decision out of his hand.

'I think I can guess what is going on in that head of yours' she said confidently. 'You are

173

planning to go to Wrex Tower tonight but you are not going without me!' JC briefly chuckled before leaning forward and clasping her hands tightly.

'I can't believe how amazing you have been Maisie. To be honest, I'm not sure that I could have approached this situation so positively without your support.' Maisie's grin reappeared.

'That's what friends are for. Now why don't you hurry up and get changed.' JC rose from his bed a little too quickly and felt a twinge in his side. The pain quickly subsided, but it served as a useful reminder of his fragile state. When he returned from the bathroom, doubts about enlisting Maisie in the venture were once again racing through his mind:

'Are you are absolutely certain about this Maisie?' She smiled.

'Yes…. but only after you have answered one question.' He nodded.

'Have you told Amanda any of this?'

'No.'

'Okay, let's go.'

****

The icy breeze that struck JC when he took his first tentative steps from the hospital left him feeling like he had been administered smelling salts. His strength was returning at an accelerated rate and his movements instinctive for the first time since his recovery. The sight that awaited him in the outside world was not what he had expected but on reflexion it was what he had become accustomed too. He witnessed an agitated driver beeping his horn at a paramedic who had carelessly parked his ambulance, thus causing congestion. A woman with a badly damaged ankle being assisted by a courteous passer-by. An act the Samaritan regretted when he discovered that his *damsel in distress* was inebriated and bestowed with a vicious tongue.

Most harrowing of all he observed a young couple hurriedly exiting a taxi with anxious expressions on their faces. The man cradling a motionless infant in his arms while the woman desperately asked for directions. These were scenarios that could have occurred in any major city. But this was not a typical City. This was Friday night at a London Hospital. London. A city that daunted yet beguiled him at the same time. It was life as he knew it. Once seated in Maisie's car the reality of their situation finally dawned on her.

'We can't be sure they have your friend, after all why would they allow him to be taken to hospital to receive treatment and then recapture him?'

'I know.' He responded promptly, 'I have thought of nothing else since I realised that Lenny was still alive, but if Gloria's disciples did not kidnap him then where else could he be? It has to be them.'

'But are you sure it will be safe to enter Wrex Tower? Won't they have stepped up security since the ritual failed?' JC smiled to himself.

Maisie's pangs of anxiety made her all the more endearing.

'Well, they already have Lenny and I am barely out of a coma. I imagine the last thing they would be expecting right now is a hostile visitor.'

His words had a calming effect, and ensured that the car journey was spent in good spirits. Conversation centred around their wonderful summer together, when life seemed a lot simpler. There was relatively little traffic to slow their progress so they were able to reach their destination in good time. Maisie had, under advisement from JC, parked two blocks away.

'Okay Maisie, I'm going in. Make sure that the car doors are locked securely after I'm gone. You can't be too careful this time of night, and I may be gone a while.' Maisie eased back in her seat.

'Oh, don't worry about me. This is the perfect opportunity to complete the crossword I started two days ago. It's in here somewhere; now go get 'em Jase!' Jase? He was called Jase once before but from whom he could not remember. It was a long time ago and his memory since coming out of the coma has been a little sketchy. He could recall not liking the alias, but now coming from Maisie it sounded quite pleasant.

He looked back to deliver a reassuring smile. It was only then that he realised Maisie had upgraded her car. She was now driving a 2013 Volkswagen beetle. It was re-sprayed pink with large rose petal imprints on the doors and bonnet. It was impossible to determine the colours of the petals in the dark, but they were most likely blue and green.

'Oh that is so Maisie.' He turned and smiled contentedly to himself as he strode towards Wrex Tower, but the nearer he came to the building, the more he was consumed by memories of his last ill-fated visit.

****

The security guard smiled and commented on the weather as JC displayed his identity card. So, the first hurdle was effortlessly negotiated but as JC stood anxiously by the elevator he noticed the suitably positioned security cameras and wondered if additional systems had been installed since he was smuggled out of the building. The elevator was taking an eternity to arrive. The security guard tried to strike up conversation by commenting on how unusually busy it had been for a Friday evening. Now it all seemed too easy. As though he was being lured into a trap.

As he entered the elevator he felt physically weak. The strenuous effort to get this far was taking its toll. He looked at himself in the glass panelled mirror. *Why do they always install glass panelled mirrors*? He was startled by his pale complexion. Beads of perspiration were pouring down his face. The resemblance between himself and his father was all too apparent once again.

For some unknown reason he was reminded of the moment he discovered his parents were divorcing. The old man; a habitual womaniser went on to marry a young filly barely out of her teens. The inevitable happened, and when she eventually left him penniless and alone he was surprisingly accepting of his fate.

'But I'm not like him. Never have been and never will be!' It dawned on him how thoughts of his father surfaced only in times of doubts over his own convictions. When he was struggling to maintain the façade. The elevator doors opened to reveal that he was still on the ground floor. *He had forgotten to press the elevator floor button.* The security guard immediately stood up from his seat, with walkie-talkie in hand and a puzzled expression on his face. JC smiled nervously. The doors automatically closed once again, which was JC's queue to openly express his anxiety.

'Crap... crap. Right must focus. Press the button. Which floor... which...three!'

The third floor. As the elevator doors opened he expected to be confronted by security guards, waiting to detain him. There was no-one. But there was a light on in Kate's office. Kate Pritchard; the woman who had lured him into the supposedly defective elevator before plying him with champagne laced with a sedative. The woman who condemned him to a twisted existence that should have endured for all eternity. Nothing would give him greater pleasure than confronting her and, one way or another, obtaining the information he needed.

He became aware for the first time of the disparities between Kate's office and those of her peers. Kate's was much larger and fitted with a glass door. Both windows and doors had an unusual blue tint which made the occupant appear bulkier than they actually were. On this occasion the occupant was most definitely Kate, and she was pacing back and forth with phone in hand. JC decided to enter the room after the phone call had ended, but before he could do so a tall slender figure - that he had hitherto failed to notice - stood up from his chair and moved swiftly towards her. He held her tightly, placing his left hand around her waist while his right hand gently caressed her cheeks. They indulged in a passionate kiss. JC had to act quickly before the situation became awkward. He placed his hand on the door handle, but then panicked. It took a loud groan from Kate to focus his mind once again. He hurriedly swung open the door.

'Hello Kate. I think you have a lot of explaining to do!' The couple stood motionless without making a sound, but it was JC who was most surprised. The man that Kate had been cavorting with was Marvin Webb, Head of Development. The young pup who had chaired JC's interview panel! It was now apparent to him how someone so young, unpopular and ill-equipped for leadership had acquired a key management role. JC's ego had been dented, but he was determined to concentrate on the issues that brought him to Wrex Tower in the dead of night.

'I want answers Kate and I want them now!' Kate still exhibited a startled expression as she hastily fastened the buttons on her blouse.

'Is that you JC? My God you look terrible! What on earth are you doing here?' Even when taken unawares Kate was determined to take control of the situation. JC was adamant that she would not do so.

'I need to speak to you alone' he turned to Marvin. 'Now if you please.'

Kate signalled Marvin to stay put, but then she noticed that JC was gingerly holding his ribs as he paced languidly around the office. He was too weak to pose a physical threat.

'I'll speak to you later Marvin' she said nonchalantly, 'but do not leave the building. I may still be in need of your assistance before the nights over.'

Marvin sighed before leaving. He intentionally left the door ajar but JC - watching his every move - slammed the door shut.

'Now Kate, first question. Why did you drug me?' An amused expression emerged on Kate's face.

'I don't know what you are talking about! Your injuries must be affecting you more than you realise.'

JC grimaced before slowly making his way to the chair that Marvin had recently vacated. It could have been the prospect of finally confronting his subjugator, or merely the act of *taking the weight off his feet* which transformed his disposition, but the moment he was seated JC's sharpness of mind returned.

'There is no point in denying it,' he said confidently. 'I have spoken to Gloria… Suzy, or whatever you want to call her about the crossing the bridge process. She told me everything.' Kate's eyes lit up with excitement.

'Really? So it does actually work! Tell me what was it like?' He looked at her contemptuously.

'You left me for dead! Well as good as. My whole life changed… ruined. I had to endure an existence that I detested with a woman that I…I.'

JC found himself lost for words. He was relieved when Kate intervened.

'I know you must hate me right now but you cannot begin to understand the pressure I was under. In a way you ought to be thanking me really.'

'Thanking you…. for what?' Savouring the moment Kate settled comfortably in her high back leather chair before continuing.

'Who do you think took you to the hospital and made sure you received proper medical attention?' Visibly shaken by Kate's admission JC leaned back in his chair, firmly gripping both arm rests.

'Why on earth would you do that?' Kate laughed out loud.

'I'm not a total bitch you know. I did what I was obligated to do and ensured that you participated in the ritual. Fortunately for you the process takes time, and an opportunity arose for us to get you out of there undetected.'

'Us? You and Marvin?'

'Yes.' JC loosened his grip on the arm rests.

'Thank you,' he said earnestly. 'You risked a great deal for me.'

'That's alright' she replied calmly. 'After all it's the least I could do…. for the father of my child.'

****

JC was convinced that she was referring to Gloria's offspring, Abigail and had inexplicably muddled her words. But he hesitated. This was not the time for uncertainty. It was important that every word she uttered was processed and substantiated before moving on.

'If you are referring to the daughter that I had with Gloria then don't worry. I know all about her and I will do my best to be a good father to her. Especially now that Gloria has passed away.'

Kate did not reply. Instead she stood up and walked slowly towards the window. Looking out onto the bright lights of the City. When she eventually turned to face him her expression had changed. She appeared melancholy; there was an air of vulnerability about her.

'I see Gloria did not tell you everything.' JC simply gazed in her direction. There was a blank expression on his face. Knowing what was to come made him feel angry; disgusted with himself, but he needed to hear it.

'My daughter. Cheryl. The girl in that photo is your daughter.'

Kate pointed to a photo on the wall, but there was no need for him to examine it. It was a photo he had been drawn to on his first day at work. He remembered thinking how cute the young girl was, only now he could see that she looked so much like him at that age. The same large welcoming eyes, round face and cute button nose. She continued.

'I will spare you the details of our brief relationship. I don't want to go into it and you probably won't even remember if I told you. As you can see it had a profound effect on…well, the rest of my life.' JC sighed and shook his head.

'Are there any more children that I should know about?'

'Not that I am aware of, but who knows how many of your ex-partners had taken the morning after pill, had abortions, or even had your baby but just slipped away quietly. Never to be seen again.' JC clung tightly to the arm rests once more.

'So that's what this is all about,' he said dispassionately. 'Revenge for my past sins.'

'Yes!' She replied brusquely. 'That is exactly what this is all about. Payback. When Gloria initially accrued her wealth it was all about the money. The power. Making sure she was in a position where she could never be hurt again. All that changed when she was allowed access into the male-dominated world of the freemasons and their ancient rituals. Even then she had no real interest in their peculiar activities until she learned of the Crossing the Bridge ceremony.

You see, Gloria had never forgiven you for moving on with your life, yet she still loved you. If she could not have you then no-one else would. The ritual would either prove effective and you would spend an eternity in her company or you would die together…evidently it did not go according to plan.'

'I understand that' he said anxiously,' but what still confuses me is why you took part in the process? Particularly as I am the father of your child.

'Because I owe her.' She immediately replied.

'We all owe her. Gloria spent years tracking down your ex-girlfriends. Women you have treated with contempt over the years. She recruited a number of us. Gave us good jobs. Careers. She was particularly benevolent to me. I think it was because I was also bringing up your child. Before I met Gloria I was working as a secretary for a crummy law firm. Look at me now!' JC emitted a wry smile.

'That explains why so many of the female staff look familiar. Although I met Amy after she was employed here.'

'I know. That really annoyed Gloria. She asked me to investigate and nip it in the bud, but fortunately for me you did your usual thing and left her hanging.'

'So you did it all for the money?' His retaliatory remark was flatly ignored.

'Gloria wanted as many of us as possible to share in the moment. I did too to an extent, but thankfully I came to my senses in time. I hate what you have done to so many of us but that does not mean you should suffer indefinitely because of it.'

JC had one more question to ask, but for him it was probably the most important of the night.

'Where is Lenny?' Kate broke into fits of laughter.

'Lenny. That fool! He was taken in by Gloria from the start. I have no idea where he is. I have not seen him since Gloria died.'

'Is it possible that he is being held here without your knowledge?'

'I suppose it is. Security around the basement has been tightened since you absconded and now that Gloria is no longer around I am not always kept in the loop.' He momentarily hesitated before putting his cards on the table.

'I have to rescue Lenny.....destroy this so-called tree of life. I am one of the few that has returned from the other side. There has to be a reason for that and the only one I can think of is that I am supposed to end this unjust practice. But I will need your help to do it. Will you help me?'

Kate thought long and hard before responding.

'You are asking a lot JC, but Gloria is gone and I detest that tree. My loyalty was to Gloria not the Company. Marvin and I will aid you on two conditions. Firstly, you do not involve the police. If this organisation survives with its reputation intact then there is a chance that I will come out of this in a much stronger position.'

'And the second?'

'You are on your own. I will provide you with a way in and a weapon to destroy the tree. If possible I will find out the location of your friend too, but you have to do the job yourself. Are we agreed?'

'Yes,' he immediately replied, 'we are agreed.'

14

Having woken from his first restful night's sleep since coming out of a coma, JC lazily turned onto his side to face the bay window and for a brief moment he had no idea where he was. His heart skipped a beat when he realised that someone was lying beside him. Motionless. Although she had her back to him he could tell by the curvature of the body that it was a beautifully formed woman; but who was it? Natural light effortlessly penetrated the flimsy white curtains to shed light onto their surroundings, which enabled him to recollect salient details. The curtains along with the plain white bed sheets and pillow cases were purchased from a market stall in Camden Town but the curtains were considered *not fit for purpose* and dispensed with; or so he thought. The woman stirred and the sheet slowly drifted from her neck and shoulders to reveal short dark hair and lightly tanned skin. His suspicions were confirmed. He was back home in his own bed with Amanda. His feelings of anxiety disappeared.

It had been two days since his daring return to Wrex Tower. Until that point he perceived the edifice itself and all associated with it as reprehensible and a genuine threat to everyone he ever cared for. Now all that had changed. Thanks to Kate many of the questions that were keeping him awake at nights had been answered. In addition she provided him with a detailed map of the Wrex Tower basement, highlighting the most likely places where Lenny might be held hostage. But her prognosis for his friend was not so good:

> 'I have never heard of anyone other than the host surviving the return journey from the other side and even that is rare. There were rumours of one recipient surviving for a few days. That was in the early nineteenth century. A woman returned to fatally wound the Count who had ensnared her before she too succumbed. Unfortunately the mind becomes dependent on the host and is rapidly worn out by the effort of working independently once again.'

It had been four days since JC emerged from his coma. A short time for him but an eternity for someone in Lenny's position. On a positive note Lenny was showing signs of making a recovery prior to being abducted, and he would have been buoyed by the knowledge that his special relationship with JC had stood the test of time. It was also fortuitous that JC had the opportunity to inform Lenny of Amy's true feelings towards him. Perhaps these combined factors would provide him with the motivation to survive.

'Are you okay JC?' Amanda's softly spoken words took JC by surprise. She still had her back to him and had showed no signs of being awake.

'Uh, yes I'm fine. It's just that for a moment there I'd forgotten I was discharged from hospital.' Amanda chuckled to herself before turning to face him.

'Discharged from hospital? More like thrown out! Honestly I don't know what you were thinking, going for late night trips without consent while recovering from a coma. Well it's like the doctor said, 'if you are healthy enough to go for late night walks then you are healthy enough to be discharged.'

JC failed to respond, his thoughts disturbed by the vibration of his mobile phone. It could be the text message he had been waiting for.

'I'm going downstairs,' he said brusquely. 'I think I'll make myself a coffee and a full English. Interested?'

'Uhm..Yeah, sure. You sound a bit more like your old self today.' Once again he saw no reason to respond to her comment.

'See you in the kitchen, Amanda. Take your time though as I'll probably be awhile.'

On entering the kitchen JC switched the kettle on. A meaningless gesture. All he wanted to do was check his text message. It was as he hoped, a message from Kate. It read:

> 'Tonight's the night. Everything will be ready, as discussed. Make sure you arrive at <u>exactly 10.45pm</u>. Don't forget if anything goes wrong you're on your own. Delete this text after you have read it.

Be careful JC xx

So far so good. Kate was sticking to her side of the agreement and he was mentally prepared to do what was necessary. There was just one more thing that needed to be done. He could hear Amanda humming to herself on the landing. Soon she will be joining him in the kitchen. It had been such a long time since she seemed so content with life. Somehow their relationship was back on track. Where it had been before he had unwittingly participated in the crossover ritual. No, before that. Soon after she returned to work following maternity leave. Since then he has had to endure long, agonising periods of uncertainty, precipitated by Amanda's terrible mood swings and signs of an affair that never was. This made what he had to do now all the more difficult. In the blink of an eye Amanda's feelings of contentment will be shattered. But he had no choice. It was time to be frank with her.

****

JC slowly sipped his cup of coffee. He had lost his appetite. Amanda could be heard pacing between the bedroom and bathroom. She had gone from humming to singing her favourite song.

'So,' he mumbled to himself, 'she finally remembered the lyrics.'

As he waited for Amanda to join him JC's thoughts turned to the moment he walked out of Wrex Tower two days ago, following his poignant encounter with Kate. He was in a daze, unable to comprehend the gravity of the situation. The sight of Maisie's eye-catching vehicle proved a welcome distraction. Maisie was asleep in the driver's seat, snoring lightly. Her head resting snugly against a small pink and blue striped pillow. In her lap was an old newspaper which was neatly folded in the middle. The crossword was barely visible under the flared sleeves of her blouse. *So she never did manage to complete it.* He watched intently as Maisie's top lip curled upwards and her eyelids flickered rapidly, as though she was busy processing information at superhuman speed. But it was a cold autumn night and like all warm-blooded creatures the need to shelter from the elements were of paramount concern. He tugged at the front passenger door and to his annoyance it opened with ease.

'Oh Maisie' he whispered to himself, 'You could have been carjacked or worse. Why do you never listen?'

JC took the newspaper from Maisie's lap and then searched around in the glove compartment until he found a pen. Less than five minutes later he gently woke her up.

'Uh…oh hi, JC. Were you gone long?'

'Long enough to get the information I needed. I will tell you all about it on the way to the hospital, but first here's your newspaper back.'

There was a look of astonishment on Maisie's face.

'Oh my goodness you have completed the crossword!' He smiled conceitedly.

'Well, you were never going to do it and as I had a few minutes to spare I thought I would fill in the blanks. I'm not just a pretty face you know.' Still staring at his handiwork Maisie's expression quickly turned to one of horror.

'Hold on. Those are the *wrong* answers! You've just randomly placed letters in the boxes. Not just a pretty face indeed, more like a lying toad.'

'Well,' He replied with a huge grin on his face,

'I didn't say it was the *correct* answers, I only said that I filled in the blanks.' Maisie playfully struck him across the face with the folded newspaper. This was followed by a friendly tussle before the inevitable kiss. This time JC was a willing participant. When they parted it was Maisie who spoke first. To his surprise there was a serious tone to her voice.

'You have got to tell Amanda.'

'What…about the kiss?'

'No. I understand why you…we did it. You needed solace and I just happened to be around, and yes we do care for each other. No, you have got to tell her about the ritual. Crossing the bridge. Lenny. Everything. Keeping secrets will do more harm than good. It's probably the only way you are going to save your relationship.' JC leaned back in his seat, and slowly nodded his head before sighing.'

'Yes, of course. You're right. I will…I promise.'

****

Amanda prided herself on being able to read JC like a book but on this occasion she was aided in her appraisal by his unusual lack of composure and surprising memory lapse. She had been looking forward to a full English breakfast but was instead served eggs on toast. The mug of coffee was supplanted by a simmering pot of tea. Although ambidextrous the way he held his beverage was also telling. The mug clasped firmly in his left hand instead of being held loosely in his favoured right hand.

'Talk to me JC. We have to be open with each other if we are to have any hope of keeping our relationship on track.'

It could have been Maisie uttering those words on her behalf. Although more upbeat lately the expression on Amanda's face served as a reminder of her continued emotional fragility. But since when did she become so desperate for reassurance? There comes a time in all intimate relationships when your status is confirmed and you become the dominant or junior partner. The latter is generally expected to make the big sacrifices in order to sustain a functioning relationship. They stop attending a much loved evening class, relocate, no longer socialise with certain friends and even neglect their careers. JC took a backseat while Amanda's career and popularity soared. He picked up the pieces when things went wrong, whether she wanted him to or not. It was not his way but he was accepting of the situation. Until now.

A curious notion crossed his mind. What if Amanda was still capable of being the same vibrant, captivating social animal who had him mesmerized within moments of their first encounter, but only in the company of Ray? If so, then the recent termination of their platonic relationship may have hastened her adverse personality transformation.

It is impossible to say what drove him to be so forthright. He intended to speak only of his entrapment at Wrex Tower and subsequent escape, but instead it all came out. That first kiss with Maisie all those months ago, the feelings he had for Suzy, the children he never knew he had and Maisie's clandestine hospital visits. Then there was that kiss. The second, meaningful kiss with Maisie. Amanda remained surprisingly calm. If she was hurt in any way she certainly did now show it.

'So now I know why you were so lenient with me. Is she my competition?'

'No. It...it happened because we...we had been seeing a lot of each other; getting closer. I needed solace and she was ...available. That's all there was to it.

'Well, it is a lot to take in. I just can't at the moment. But regarding this Maisie....well, I'll just have to say to you what you said to me. We can leave it all in the past and get on with living in the here and now. So what exactly are your plans for tonight then?

'Uh, well I intend to go to Wrex Tower...'

'What on your own?!' JC was surprised and a little overwhelmed by Amanda's heartfelt concern. Particularly coming so soon after his frank admission. He found himself lost for words.

'I'll give James a call,' she said adamantly. 'You know how he likes a bit of excitement. He will be glad to help.' JC vigorously shook his head.

'I am not allowing anyone else to get involved. Particularly someone so close to you.'

'That's not what I meant. James can drive you to Wrex Tower and then wait in the car. Nothing more. If you fail to return he can be a witness to you having entered but not leaving the building.'

'Okay, fine, but I think we should be a little flexible with the truth. It might be too much for him to handle. But you may want to ask him to bring a crossword and a comfy pillow as it could take a while.'

15

The hustle and bustle of faceless London is a far cry from the serene, parochial existence one would expect on Mainland; the largest island in the Shetlands. One of James' earliest memories, and undoubtedly the most painful was leaving London at the age of nine. Having to say good-bye to his relatives and one cousin in particular who he admired greatly because of her supreme confidence and astonishing beauty.

In the years that followed he cherished the rare occasions that he was able to meet with her or just converse on the telephone. He followed her career with great interest and pride as she achieved celebrity status. The first opportunity he had to leave home and return to London he took it. Primarily to continue his advancement in the field of commercial law, but he also had a burning desire to continue where he left off all those years ago. Develop those relationships that gave him so much joy and kept him in a positive frame of mind on those bitterly cold Shetland nights. And who better to reside near to and socialise with in England than the cousin he admired so greatly. Amanda. He would do anything for her, so he was delighted to be asked to participate in:

'A stake-out! Man this is so cool. Thanks for choosing me JC.'

'No problem James. Now you just sit here quietly and keep your eyes and ears open for anything suspicious. Remember, whatever happens you must stay in the car.'

'Yeah,' James replied excitedly 'but what if the illegal workers try to make a run for it and you need backup?'

'It won't come to that. Most of them are legit and do a wonderful cleaning job. Besides I am here to monitor their activities and not to interrogate them.'

JC loathed being deceitful to someone as impressionable as James but on this occasion he could see no other option.

'As soon as I leave close all doors and windows. See you soon.'

****

On entering Wrex Tower JC approached the security guard.

'Kate Pritchard has left a package for me, Mr Richards. It's behind the counter I believe.'

The security guard was so eager to comply that he neglected to examine JC's identity card. Once again he was off to a good start. He took the elevator to the third floor before walking the length of the hallway to the *impaired* elevator. The light was on in Kate's office. There were people present, two at least but he had to block that out of his mind and continue with the plan. He entered the code Kate had given him into the elevator key pad and the doors immediately opened. Entering the elevator evoked a myriad of emotions. A sense of fear. That was to be expected but the feeling of worthlessness; of no longer being wanted. That came as a complete surprise.

Most bizarrely of all was the anger that surfaced over his willingness to comply to Kate's demands that night. Admittedly she was still an attractive women, but she was somewhat uncouth in her pursuit of younger men. The fact that they had a child together all those years ago still baffled him. Kate was the kind of woman that he had the good sense to avoid, even during those heady days.

The elevator doors open. He is once again in the basement. The heart of the lodge. Panic sets in. In an attempt to control his emotions he took some deep breaths.

'Remain calm JC. Remain calm.' There was no one in the immediate vicinity yet JC felt as though even his thoughts might reveal his identity. *How could I have willingly come back to this place?* His thoughts turned to implementing an exit strategy, but in his heart he knew he could not leave. Lenny's life was at stake.

Sticking to the plan he turned left and entered the gentleman's toilet. Once inside he hastily occupied the nearest cubicle and opened the package. In it was a disciples robe, a ring and the handle of a weapon. A hammer or an axe perhaps? Kate had not told him which. JC allowed himself a smile. It was all going smoothly. He proceeded to put on the robe but it was too long and a little tight at the waist. *No doubt tailor made for Marvin*, he thought. After spending a few minutes making adjustments the robe still hung loosely on his hips, but at least it no longer dragged along the floor. He would need to walk a little slower than anticipated to ensure it remained that way.

On exiting the toilet he was greeted by an anxious female voice. It was Kate.

'JC. Over here, quickly.' Her presence was comforting. For the first time since entering the building he felt alert to the danger.

'What is it Kate? This is not what we planned. You are putting yourself at risk of exposure.'

Kate held tightly to his left arm while simultaneously combing the area.

'I know...I know, but things have changed. Preparations are now being made in the antechamber for another ritual which means that the Tree of Life is unguarded, now is the best time to strike. To destroy the tree forever.'

'Yes, but what about Lenny?' he replied. 'The plan was to free Lenny first before all hell broke loose.' Kate sighed.

'Yes, Lenny. I know exactly where he is being held. We will save him, I promise...but first the tree!'

It was finally happening! He had been dreaming of this moment for days and Kate was right, if he was going to destroy the tree it had to be now while he was still composed enough to do so. As they entered the chamber he noticed two people lying motionless on separate alters, less than five yards from the glistening oak tree. There was a man, perhaps in his late seventies with thin grey hair and a distinguished beard of various shades of grey. Given his frail physical appearance and gaunt complexion it was plausible that he would shortly be passing from the real world whether he wanted to or not. The woman was young, in her early twenties. There was a look of contentment, or was it acceptance etched on her beautifully sculptured face.

'I know. It is terrible,' Kate lamented. 'Another unwitting soul soon to be infused into the mind of another. That's why we need to end this now.

Beneath the woman's alter, inside a large box you will find the main part of the weapon. The axe head. Once you have attached the two parts...well, it should do the job nicely.'

He hesitated. Kate made it sound so easy but there was more to it than that. Seeing the young woman lying there made him consider all those unfortunate souls that were still merged. Still functioning at some level and still capable of harbouring dreams and aspirations. If Gloria had not made fatal errors in her planning then he would still have been one of them.

He took time to observe his surroundings. The magnificent marble pillars positioned in each corner of the room seemed strong enough to take the weight of the entire building. The beautifully carved wooden bookshelf that dominated the left hand side of the chamber was as high as the ceiling itself. Covered in dust and cobwebs the neatly positioned books and manuscripts were a sight to behold. It appeared as though they had been untouched for decades. Kate was beginning to lose patience.

'Come on JC,' she whispered, 'you've done it before, how difficult will it be to do it again?' *How did Kate know he had done it before*? He never got around to telling her how he escaped from his psychological entrapment. Could Lenny have told her? There was no time to ponder the matter but sooner or later he will push Kate for an answer.

He hurried over to the young woman's alter and knelt down to prise the axe from inside the box. To his surprise she gave out a loud groan, which temporarily distracted him. The next moment he felt a shooting pain. His arm was pinned behind his back by an unknown assailant. He now heard an all too familiar voice. The young pup himself, Marvin was taking control of the situation.

'Sorry JC, but with all due respect this was way too easy. Now get up very slowly or Max here will make this a lot more painful for you than it has to be.' JC was slowly led back to where Kate was standing.

'Well, JC here we are again.' Her tone was unreservedly condescending. 'If I didn't know any better my darling I'd swear you were falling for my lies on purpose.' *My darling*! The words grated on him, but he realised the importance of remaining civil. Once again he found himself with questions that needed to be answered.

'I suppose I am easy to read and weak,' he said timidly, 'just like…'

'Just like your father.' Kate's words, which seemed totally out of context, temporarily altered his sense of reality. It was evident that she knew more about his early life then he realised. About his father; the man not the myth.

'The truth. That is what you want more than anything JC. Am I right?' He did not respond.

'The truth is that we had never formally met until recently. I used to see you fooling around with your friends in our hometown and just like all the other girls, I fancied you like crazy. I was a lot older than you. In fact you were in your final year at school and just turned sixteen and I'd just finished University.

We were from different worlds but I thought if I could just get close to your parents it might give me the edge over the other girls, but your dad saw things differently. He took advantage of the situation, manipulated me into sleeping with him and eventually I became pregnant with his child. Yes...my daughter is really your sister! Kate stopped for a moment to assess the impact of her disclosure. JC said nothing. He felt nothing. She continued.

'I was then discarded. Your father treated me like a common whore who got what she deserved, and your mother.... Well, she knew what had been going on but never mentioned it. In fact she never spoke to me again! That is why I became Gloria's favourite. She thought of me and my daughter as your family and not a rival for your affections. I was someone who, just like her had suffered more than most at the hands of the Richards lineage.'

'Then why am I here?' he said calmly, 'if you knew anything about me you'd know that I despised my father.' She smiled broadly.

'I know, and to your credit you have changed in recent times. Become the man I knew you could be. Gloria and I both noticed it. That is why she thought the time was right for the crossover. I could not allow it to succeed because after all this time I still love you.'

Surprised by her declaration JC turned to face Marvin; her lover. Marvin was clearly upset but tried desperately not to show it. Kate derived a good deal of pleasure from observing JC's response.

'Marvin and I are adults just having a fling, and a wonderful experience it has been too.' She was toying with both men now but only JC was willing to call her bluff.

'Okay Kate, I'm glad that you've got it all off of your chest. Now if you immediately release me I'll say no more about it.'

'Let you go?' His heart sank as she responded.

'Tonight is a very special occasion JC. Preparations are already underway for our cross over. But don't worry my darling, this time there will be no mistakes. No turning back. We will soon be together forever in our own perfect world.'

****

There was a look of uncertainty in Marvin's eyes. He was reluctant to administer the injection, yet for some reason was compelled to do as Kate instructed. The only question was why?

'Would you like me to lay on one of the altars Marvin, while you prepare to end my existence?'

Marvin's failure to respond did not deter JC. His only hope was to somehow get into his head and hope that his self-doubts will consume him.

'You clearly have strong feelings for Kate, and it is obvious that the two of you belong together. I can't understand why you would want to go through with this. Condemn her to a life that is not worth living with a man you clearly dislike.'

'It's her decision not mine.' A response.

'Oh, I see.' JC surmised, 'Then it's all about money and status. No doubt you will get a big pay rise and yet another promotion for your troubles. I suppose that is more important than helping the woman you love.'

'Shut your mouth!'

In truth it was easy for one so adept at toying with people's emotions to localise the younger man's tipping point. Marvin lashed out, his blow sending JC hurtling to the floor. JC's lip was cut, he was dazed and confused but he had bought himself some time.

'You idiot…,' Kate exclaimed, 'If you have damaged his intellect in any……'

The wailing sound that interrupted Kate's verbal assault took everyone by surprise. Still unable to get to his feet JC was the last to witness a hooded individual dressed in a disciples robe, savagely hacking at the tree of life. He was utilising the axe that Kate's disciple's had foolishly left unattended.

'Nooo! Stop him!' Kate's screams of anguish stunned her disciples into action, but before they could reach their target it was clear that substantial damage had been done.

The tree shook violently; much like a human being would respond when hit by a bullet at point blank range. All those present would never forget what happened next, for it would impose on their thoughts and plague their dreams for years to come. It was the sound of a thousand souls being prised from their notion of utopia and a thousand more being released from eternal torment. The tree itself rapidly changed in colour and texture; from glass to a more natural appearance, then to an obscure charcoal state. A portent to its unparalleled suffering. Finally, in its glass form once again, it shimmered one last time before lazily toppling to the ground and shattering. Narrowly missing its prostrate assailant.

A hooded woman who had gone unnoticed by all who were present quickly rushed over to tend to the assailant. As she anxiously called for help her hood fell backwards, revealing her all too familiar features.

'JC...JC come quick. I think he's dying!' This time he immediately recognised her. It was Amy. The last friendly face he saw before the cross over. Which meant that the assailant could only be:

'Lenny! Oh my God. It's Lenny!' JC rushed over to where his friend lay and placed his right hand under his head.

'Hi Lenny, so you made it back.' Lenny's smile was instantly followed by a grimace.

'I'm b-back... but not for long.' Amy screamed at Kate and her disciples. Imploring them to call for help.

'Don't b-bother Amy. It's too late for me. No s-strength left.' Lenny strained to look into the eyes of the two people that meant so much to him.

'What a w-way to go. Helping my best friend.'

Tears rolled down JC's cheeks. He could only watch as Lenny struggled to articulate his thoughts.

'It's good to see you once m-more. Look after each o-other and those who mean the most to you.....au r-revoir.' And with that impassioned plea Lenny was no more.

The silence was broken by Kate.

'You and your lady friend can leave now. I'll sort this mess out with the police.'

'W-What!?'

'Don't sound so shocked JC. It's over. Lenny had obviously been staying with bird-brain here, plotting to come to your rescue, so there is no case of kidnapping to answer to and now that the tree has been destroyed you have no hard evidence against us whatsoever.' Neither Amy nor JC cared to respond. Kate continued.

'Look, I am not totally heartless. I'm sorry for your loss but Lenny was trespassing and caused significant damages. It is unfortunate that he died due to the extent of his previous injuries.

Now if you two do not leave right now I will have you both arrested for trespassing.' JC chuckled at the irony.

'You are forgetting that officially we both still work here.'

'I hadn't forgotten,' Kate replied 'and if you leave right now you might still be able to keep your jobs.' Amy slowly nodded while JC looked at Kate in a quizzical manner.

'Oh don't look so worried JC, I will no longer be your line manager. I've gone up in the world now! And now that the tree has been destroyed you will no longer have to fear being sentenced to an eternity with yours truly. You don't have to decide now. Think about it.'

Think about it? So that was it. The tree had been destroyed, Lenny and Gloria had passed away and the how and why's had been explained. Unfortunately life has never been that simple. One part of his life may have been clarified but all he could foresee, aside from a lengthy period of mourning, were more questions that needed to be answered. The only difference was that now he held some of the answers to those questions. Amanda, Maisie, Amy, the children and even Kate. After all they had been through the least they owed each other was total honesty, and for his part JC would endeavour to resolve the salient issues in his life as soon as possible.

Epilogue

16

The volume on the stereo was raised higher than JC would have liked, so he remained by the front door. At least then he could hear the doorbell when it rang. He was joined by his old friend Print Room Pete, now simply referred to as Pete.

'I just don't understand why you've been so stressed out this evening, the party's going really well.'

JC responded with a fleeting smile. Engaging in conversation would distract him from his happy place. Recollecting the days when he and his *clubbing companions* participated in nights out on the town without a care in the world. Ever since the passing of Lenny, he could only recall the good times. Laughing until his tummy ached, eating heartily after a good night out, successfully conversing with women. In reality pleasurable and disagreeable experiences transpired in relatively equal measures but as the finer details of their escapades faded from his memory the need to fill the void with inspirational moments proved irresistible.

The doorbell rang. JC welcomed his guests. Thoughts of those happy days were pushed into the background but the warm inner glow they generated remained. As the guests shuffled past JC turned to his friend.

'Thanks for coming at such short notice Pete. I know that I have said it before but it is really great to see you again.' He was surprised to see

Pete blush. Even now he was a little overawed by the mere presence of JC.

'Thanks for the invite, and for telling me the truth about Lennie's death. I am still finding it all so hard to believe.'

'I know. But you have to admit that it's typical of him to pass away like that. He was always a bit of a drama queen.' They chuckled in a reverential manner.

'So JC, how long have you been working at Wrex Tower now?'

'Eight months next Thursday.' The response was instantaneous. After all how could he forget the day he began working for an organisation that had such a profound effect on his life.

'Yeah,' Pete replied enthusiastically, 'it's just as I thought it would be. You've got everything going for you. Wonderful house, great job, gorgeous partner and three beautiful children. Tell me JC, after all the women you have been with, why her? I mean… is she really the one?'

'I wouldn't be marrying her if she wasn't.' It suddenly dawned on him that Pete had posed the question not out of curiosity, but for guidance. Perhaps he too had strong feelings for someone.

'You know what Pete, I think I knew from the first moment I met her, but I tried to fight it. It was all so new and different from how I had felt in the past. I had a need…a craving to be with her that would not go away. Being with her meant having to accept what I was becoming and caste aside who I once was. If that makes any sense to you.'

'Yes it does,' Pete replied 'and I suppose that's why you've cut your hair short and dyed it black? You're kind of making a statement of your commitment?'

JC took a step back so that he could look at Pete with fresh eyes. He had previously considered such an insightful remark beyond his capabilities.

'I hadn't thought of it in those terms before but yes, maybe it is. I receive less attention from women because of it, and I'm fine with that. I am more at ease with myself.'

The doorbell rang. It was Kate with her daughter Cheryl, JC's half-sister and a tall be-spectacled gentleman. He was formally dressed and a lot older than Kate's usual suitors.

'Hello JC, this is Hans Bakker, a..uh...business acquaintance.' The two men shook hands. 'Can you be a darling Hans, and hand the bags to JC. The twin's birthday presents are not labelled but they are coloured coded so they should be able to work out who gets what. I trust they are enjoying their birthday party?'

'Absolutely,' JC replied. 'This is my good friend Pete.'

'Ah, Print Room Pete. Your colleague and drinking companion who you first met while working at North Sacs International.' Kate's comment took both men by surprise.

'Relax JC. My recollection is based entirely on research initiated on Gloria's behalf. I also have a wonderful memory that borders on photographic, so I never forget a thing. That's all in the past now.'

JC smiled and led his guests into the kitchen for beverages. On the surface he seemed okay but in reality he was annoyed with himself. It had been months since the negative emotions that were all too common at the time of the crossover had manifested. Since then he had begun to enjoy life and knuckled down to work to the extent that he was recently rewarded with a promotion. The only person to suspect his inner torment was Abigail, the teenage daughter he never knew he had until recently.

'Hi dad, it looks like you could do with a hug.'

Abigail resembled her mother, Gloria. JC was amazed at his ability to come to terms with that fact. There was no doubt in his mind that Abigail should be brought up with her siblings, but he was unable to determine if his decision was predicated on paternal instincts or a guilty conscience. Guilt for his part in the death of her mother.

'Er,..Abby,' he said coyly, 'thanks for the hug sweetie. Do you mind if I ask you a question?'

'Sure go ahead.'

'Well...are you happy here?' She responded without hesitation.

'Yes, absolutely.'

'Well, it must be difficult for you on a day like this. Your brother and sister, who you hardly know are getting all the attention and all the presents while most people here are still wondering who you are.'

'At least they *are* wondering who I am' she replied, 'and at least I now feel like I exist! When I was living with mum it was just the two of us and she was always angry about something. We rarely went anywhere together and when we did it was always to do the things she wanted. I do miss her terribly but now I have a father who is concerned about my lack of social life and always wondering if I am happy at school. A future step-mother who is great fun, warm and caring, and siblings who are pleased to have a big sister who they could talk to about music, clothes and the latest IPad's. Now ask me again if I am happy?'

JC presented a broad grin as he hugged his daughter once more. He decided then and there that it did not matter why he had brought Abigail into the fold. She had become an integral part of his family within a short period of time, and they all loved her deeply. It was quite simply the right thing to do.

****

The house was heaving with guests. Numerous relatives. Some he had not seen in years and others it seemed he would never be rid of. Most of the guests were people he had known for less than a year. Employees at Wrex Tower and just like him in their early thirties and in committed relationships with parental responsibilities.

'Daddy' Jacob shouted in frustration, 'The doorbell is ringing again. Shall I get it?'

'Okay Tiger, but why don't I come with you just in case it's an ogre who has not eaten today.'

'Ahh, Daddy!' Jacob could not help but laugh out loud as he skipped all the way to the front door.

'It's Mummy!' he shouted excitedly. 'You're late mummy, but that's okay.'

Amanda produced a glowing smile before stooping down to hug Jacob. As she did so she looked up at JC and winked. A feeling of déjà vu overwhelmed him. Amanda's confidence and poise had returned. Her ability to magically transform the atmosphere of a room by her presence alone was there for all to see. Her hair was growing back and her natural hair colour had been restored, augmented by even lighter highlights. Amanda's dress sense too - which he had used as a barometer of her mood during those dark times – was reminiscent of their courting days.

'Hello JC. How are you mate?' She was not alone. The deep bellowing voice that seemed to form a trail of its own behind Amanda belonged to Ray, her new partner.

'I'm Fine thanks Ray. It's good to see you both. Come on through.'

After giving the twins their birthday presents Amanda and Ray wasted no time in seeking out the dance area. JC watched intently as they moved as one to the beat of the music and it suddenly occurred to him that breaking up does not have to be a blame game. Their relationship was failing. They both desperately needed to develop as individuals; reach the next phase in their lives, but were afraid of the consequences.

The delay in making what was the only rational decision proved costly. It was Amanda who suffered the most, becoming less vocal and more distant as time went by. He could not recall who first suggested a separation but once it was out there in the open they promptly thrashed out their main areas of concern in the shortest time possible.

Amanda stayed at a hotel for a few weeks – for appearance sake - before moving into Ray's apartment in Wimbledon. Which meant that JC could continue to reside in the family home as the primary carer for the children. Now, four months later it was almost impossible to tell who was happier. Nevertheless for the briefest of moments JC was envious of Ray; his successor. The early stages of a relationship with Amanda could never be equalled. It was a time when she performed at her peak. In high-spirits and eager to toy with her prey. When she enticingly revealed just that little bit more about herself with each passing day.

His thoughts were interrupted by Pete and Amy who were giggling away to each other. The pair had met briefly once before. The night JC enticed her away from Lenny. On that occasion they hardly spoke. Today they were getting on like a house on fire.

'There's someone waiting outside for you JC' Amy said mischievously. 'She's waiting by her car and guess what? She seems a little upset,

215

which is funny because I didn't think she did the whole upset drama thing. Anyway, have you guessed who it is yet?'

JC desperately searched through the pockets of his cream and blue coloured jacket - a present from his fiancé - for his mobile phone.

'Oh no! My phone is on silent. She sent me a text five minutes ago. There's a car boot full of refreshments that needs bringing in. Can you give me a hand Pete?'

He had not seen her for three hours but it felt like three days. It was his love for her that had given him the strength to endure his darkest days during the last eight months and to think positively on the future.

Not wishing to keep her waiting any longer he strode swiftly towards the front door, skilfully avoiding conversation seekers. When he finally set eyes on her standing beside the boot of her vehicle a wave of excitement mixed with an inner feeling of warmth consumed him. It was always that way in her company. Ignoring her hostile facade he pulled her close to him, and as he did so the tension that had governed every fibre of her being melted away.

'Oh I do love you Jase, even though you can be a pain at times.'

JC relinquished his hold on her and took a step back, so that he could look deep into her eyes.

'I love you too, Maisie.'

She instinctively knew he had never said those words with such passion before. To anyone. It was a pivotal moment in their relationship. They had been living together for just over two months and up until that moment Maisie had been feeling a tad overwhelmed, what with living in JC's family home, with his children and the memories of Amanda. But with those five little words she suddenly felt assured; as though she was finally coming home. With Pete in attendance additional dialogue on the subject was not an option, so Maisie decided to make light of the situation.

'Well I imagine you would not have asked Sally-Ann and I to move in with you if you did not love me now would you! Although I'm sure I could have done a lot better for myself, but I was tired of holding out for Mr Right.'

'Well,' he quickly retorted, 'I was holding out for a Miss Right, but I figured I was on the *right* track when I met you. Do you get it? Right track.'

The light-hearted banter continued unabated during the unloading. When Maisie and JC finally made their way into the kitchen they were given a warm welcome by the children. JC's family, old and new joined him in the lounge and as he and Maisie danced alongside Amanda and Ray he wondered if life could get any better than this.

A cursory glance around the room confirmed all was well but for some reason his gaze reverted back to Kate and Hans. They were seated by the fireplace. Kate was, unsurprisingly the main contributor to their discussion. JC did wonder why she occasionally emitted signs of anxiety. But, not wishing to detract from the harmonious ambience of the evening he put it down to the usual teething problems associated with a blossoming relationship. Particularly one between two powerful, strong-willed administrators.

While it was true that Kate and Hans had been inseparable all night it was not for the reason that JC and his guests had assumed.

'Well Kate' Hans whispered. 'I am glad to finally set eyes on the man that has been at the centre of your world all these years, but I have to admit I was expecting someone a little more…dashing.'

'Don't be so quick to judge,' she replied defensively. 'This is not his usual look. He is currently going through a phase. You know… wanting to please others. Trying to be all things to all men and change his true nature. It never lasts.' She looked up at JC. 'In his case I will see to that.'

Hans looked pensively at her.

'What you are asking for is impossible, my dear. I have been on the phone for two days now trying to persuade the leaders of our most honourable and beloved lodge in Norway to part with the ancient *giver av liv* …ah sorry, *giver of life*. They just won't do it. You failed to stop one tree being destroyed, they simply will not trust you with the sole remaining Tree of Life.'

Kate gently stroked his cheek before delivering an alluring smile.

'Then I will just have to double…..no triple my offer. After all that's what this is all about, isn't it Hans? This ….foreplay. It's all down to money, and since Gloria's demise I now have lots of it.   One way or another it is going to happen. It is inevitable and we both know it. Sooner or later JC and I will cross over the bridge and remain there together for all eternity.'

End

www.ingramcontent.com/pod-product-compliance
Lightning Source LLC
Chambersburg PA
CBHW030449250626
47154CB00003BA/1188

* 9 7 8 0 9 9 3 5 1 1 7 4 5 *